# The Velvet Elite:

## Unforgettable Love

by
Emmy Waterford

c2018
Waterford Publishing

THE VELVET ELITE: Unforgettable Love

Written by Emmy Waterford
c2018 Waterford Publishing Co. www.emmywaterford.com

This book is dedicated to my husband and our precious memories.

With a grateful heart, I love you.

# CHAPTER 1
## At the Intersection

My fingers gripped the leather steering wheel, my wrists resting on the cool steel spokes. It pushed against my forehead, cool breeze whipping through my hair. The window was down slightly or possibly broken. I woke up slowly, forcing my eyes open and focusing on the mountain terrain upended in front of me. Pushing myself away from the steering wheel and looking around, I strained to grasp what must have happened. *Did I pull over? Did I fall asleep at the wheel?* I focused on the big green rectangle posted just a few yards ahead: *San Francisco 54 miles south, San Merhita 7 miles north.*

Regaining my senses, I rolled down my squeaky and dusty window. I needed fresh air. The breeze blew in, sucking the air out of my lungs. I smelled the salt of the nearby ocean breeze, so I knew I couldn't be far from the water. I closed my eyes as I inhaled deeply. I looked into my rearview mirror to see the funnel of brown dust bellowing behind an approaching truck. It pulled up beside me and the driver leaned over to roll down the passenger side window.

"Are you okay, miss?" Still confused and a little embarrassed, I nodded. He held up his hand. "Stay right there, I'm coming around." I bobbed my head in agreement, looking around the inside of my car for clues as to what had happened.

Everything was intact. There was no blood anywhere, and I didn't feel any broken bones. I hadn't crashed into anything, at least I knew that. The Good Samaritan walked to my window. "Can I help you?" He repeated his questions and I tried to answer him. He seemed worried, and that began to worry me too.

A wave of heat swept through me. My heart was racing. My limbs felt foreign and uncontrolled. I raised my hands to my face. They were cold and clammy. But I felt a pendant necklace I didn't realize I was wearing. I pulled the rearview mirror down to check it, a beautiful ruby heart mounted in white gold. The good-looking man stared down at me, concern in his furrowed brow. He had an air about him, a certain glow which I couldn't quite trust or explain. Maybe it was the setting sun, but his blue eyes were stunning, nearly paralyzing me. My chin must have dropped and I could feel my cheeks burning. We shared a smile and I knew it wouldn't be the last.

He looked about ten or so years older than me. He was strong but slender, lean but not skinny. He had a graying black goatee; he was manly and ruggedly handsome. It was a look not every man could pull off. His jeans hugged him in all the right places, his white t-shirt under a plaid, long-sleeved, unbuttoned shirt seemed to flow in the breeze. His voice was as soothing as his smile was genuine, warm and inviting, his teeth white behind his smooth lips.

"Well," he said, "you seem okay. I'm glad of that." While I was enjoying his reassuring presence, I couldn't help notice that he seemed as shaken by this whole situation as I was. It couldn't have been every day he found a confused passed-out woman in a car on the side of the road.

He wiped his hand on his jeans, pushed his baseball cap up slightly, and then held out his hand to shake mine. "James."

I shaded my eyes with one hand as I shakily extended my other. "Uh, hi. Hello. I'm Elizabeth." His hand was warm and strong. His electric touch sent shockwaves throughout my entire body.

While still holding my hand, he caught my gaze. "Where were you headed?"

My mind went blank. I knew what I wanted to say, but struggled to form the words. "I'm not sure. I mean, I guess I don't remember." He cocked his head, confused or maybe even not believing me. "I must have pulled over on my way to … " I pointed slowly right, then even more slowly left … but only became more confused.

He let go of my hand and took a step back, looking at my car. "Doesn't look like you were in an accident." He glanced around. "Glad I saw you, anyway."

His cell phone rang, and he pulled it from the back pocket of his jeans. He gestured to his phone and stepped back to his truck. I continued to look around inside my car, trying to figure out what had happened. There wasn't any sign of a struggle. My seatbelt was still fastened, and my purse lay neatly on the passenger's side seat. There were no tears or rips on my skirt or my shirt, and not even a scraped knee or elbow. And the transmission was in *park*. So, I sat there, wondering, *What in the world happened?*

"Yes, everything is fine then," my rescuer said into his phone. "Sounds good … Okay, bye." He turned back to me, pocketing his phone. "I was on my way out, but it seems there's no need. Oh, I'm sorry, how rude of me." He pulled out the phone and handed it me. "Like to make a call?" I looked down at my lap and thought about his question for a moment. It felt as though I *should* make a call, just to let someone know I was okay. But I had no idea who to call, which was also quite embarrassing. James paused for a moment to allow me time to answer. "Would you like to follow me down to my house?" He pointed back the direction

7

from which he came. His eyes met mine again. "The sun is going down, and it gets foggy fairly quickly. It probably isn't the best time to be driving around on these twisting and turning roads right now."

I looked around for my phone. "Really," James said, "I'm concerned about a concussion. Come down to the house until you feel well enough to drive." I was nervous about following some strange man to his house, no matter how handsome or charming he may have been. But the alternatives weren't so sunny either, so I decided to take this Good Samaritan up on his offer.

He smiled with a knowing little chuckle. "I'm not a serial killer or anything, I promise." We both chuckled. I looked into his eyes again, feeling completely safe.

My keys were still in the ignition, so I started the car, the low fuel light flashing.

He motioned to follow him as he got into his truck. The setting sun highlighted the vineyards in the distance and the sky burst with purples and yellows and oranges. The California autumn day was chilly with a gentle breeze.

I followed him to his house, a nervous curl growing in my stomach. *Am I really doing this?* I had to ask myself. *Can I really trust this guy? I don't know him or anything about him, and nobody even knows I'm here. How did I end up here in the first place?*

I was trapped between an uncertain past and unfamiliar surroundings.

*Doesn't matter,* I reassured myself. *I'll figure it out. Just need a little time, gather my wits, maybe let this guy run me to the nearest gas station, then I'm gone!*

But the more I searched my memory for answers, the fewer I found. Not only couldn't I remember how I came to be sitting in my car on the side of the road, but I couldn't remember why I'd left home in the first place or where I'd been going.

*I must have been going somewhere, I assumed, or was I just … just driving? Was I running from a potentially harmful situation, or was I running to something or someone?*

I knew my own name, and for that I was increasingly grateful. There was no wedding ring on my finger, my only indication that I wasn't married. *But … what about my parents, my kid sister. Wait, do I even have a kid sister?*

We drove down a winding road, a crystal-clear lake in the distance, boathouses clinging to the banks. The breeze whipped through the window, refreshing, calming. And in that dizzying confusion and growing fear, I needed all the calming I could get.

# CHAPTER 2
## Dreamy Villa

Signs of a large house peeked out from behind the pines and sycamores as we rolled down the drive. Vineyards and orchards of olive trees patterned the hillsides. We drove the mile-long winding driveway, my anticipation growing. After a final turn, the house opened up in front of us — a magnificent mansion, almost a castle.

The paved drive turned to pea-gravel under the car's tires as we pulled up to the entrance. A big golden retriever ran from the side of the house, bounding around the truck. I pulled up and parked my car next to James's truck. I stepped out of my car, shading my eyes from the sun's glare to get a better look at that meticulously maintained and stunning structure.

The grounds were expertly manicured. Every flower and shrub was carefully groomed. Beautiful marguerite daisies and deep royal blue lobelia bloomed. Large, earth-toned olive jars contained beautiful shrubs and various vines. Potted plants and flowers were placed perfectly throughout his landscaping, a huge flower-and-vegetable garden in the distance on the right side of the house.

The grandiose estate soon took on a warm, cozy feel when that dog appeared, happily smiling at his owner and master. At first, I wasn't sure if this was a castle and this man the groundskeeper, but it seemed obvious that this was a humble man at home with the simpler things in life.

Even his truck was a classic model, special without being foreign or showy. "She's a beaut, eh?"

"Oh, yeah," James said, glancing at the truck. "Real

reliable, don't cost much. She's a lot of fun."

"Um, are we talking about the dog or the truck?"

James chuckled. "Maybe both." He stood and looked me right in the eye.

"Sense of humor, I like that." I put out my hand and let the dog sniff it, then gave her a playful little scratch on the head. "What's her name?"

"Layla. Y'know, after the song? " In a jangling dissonance, he sang, "Layla, you got me on my knees / Layla, I'm beggin' darlin' please."

I knew of the tune, but I still said, "Never heard of it."

"Eric Clapton?" I just shrugged and he shook his head. "You can't be that young."

"Maybe it's more about you being old."

He chuckled again. "Well, I definitely like that." He winked.

I followed James across the driveway to the flagstone sidewalk. A weathered wooden tree swing for two hung from a large olive tree to the right of the sidewalk.

There was a stone plaque on the side of the house by the front door: *Bellezza Interno.* Just when I was about to ask, James noted, "Italian for *Internal Beauty.*"

"I love that."

He smiled brightly and opened the large, mahogany door. He stepped in first. "This house has belonged to my family for generations. It's big, but it's cozy. It seems to have gotten smaller as I've gotten older, but it's definitely home."

I felt like I was stepping back in time and place, suddenly transported to Renaissance-era Tuscany. The house was quiet. We seemed to be alone in the big house. *No wife?* I wondered, *Can I really be that lucky?*

He clicked on a few lamps as he walked me further into the house, the warm light revealing new and welcoming nooks and crannies to the huge, gorgeous home. He gestured for me to join him deeper in the house. I froze, not certain if I should.

"It's okay. Please, make yourself at home. I'm going to grab some wood and start a fire. It's chilly in here. There's a phone in the kitchen if you'd like to make a call." He disappeared into the next room.

I wasn't sure if I should step any closer. I stood perfectly still in the same spot, but stuck my head out a bit when I heard him clanking things around. "James? Is there, is there a *Mrs. James?*" The background noise ceased, silence returning to the big house. He slowly strolled up to me with his hands in his front pockets. "There's no need for you to worry about that." Reading my troubled expression, he placed both hands on my shoulders. "My wife's name was Beth Ann, but she's … she's no longer with us." My heart fell.

"Oh, James, I … I'm so sorry. I shouldn't have asked."

The tender moment lingered, a bittersweet smile wriggling on his face. "I'm glad you did." James clapped to break the somber tone, then rubbed his hands together and led me into the huge kitchen. "I need to get back to that pitiful fire. Be right back." Once he was out of sight, I thumped myself on the forehead. *Oh my God, really? Really, Liz? The man is a frigging widower for crying out loud. And here you are suspecting the worst. Geez. Dumbass.*

I meandered through each room, giving each piece of furniture, each painting or portrait, every candelabra, and every piece of artwork the individual attention it deserved.

The antique tables, wall sconces, sculptures, old handmade pottery, and colorful tapestries made me feel like I was in a museum. Walking past a massive, ornate wooden-framed oval mirror, I checked my makeup and hair. I couldn't help but notice how thin I looked.

13

I turned left into the kitchen. I'd always had an obsession with kitchens, and this one did not disappoint. It was a large open-concept, with the comfortable warmth and historic beauty of a Mediterranean kitchen. A center island with a quartz countertop, three bar stools, and two wrought iron pendant lights dominated the room. The copper pots hanging in between the pendant lights were a definite reflection of what I believed was one of many talents this man possessed. The lighting was soft and relaxing, the kitchen cobblestone fireplace glowing, fire crackling, adjoining rooms waiting on the other side.

I looked down at my watch; it was nearly six o'clock. I couldn't remember the last time I had eaten. I was beginning to get a slight twinge of a headache.

Nearly out of breath, James hurriedly made his way back into the kitchen when he asked me, "Are you hungry? I hope so, because I'm starving." He gazed at me with those big beautiful eyes, winked, and then smiled. It was then that I noticed he had removed his baseball cap and changed into a faded pair of jeans and a comfy-looking beige shawl-collared sweater. The sleeves were pushed up and displayed the sexy hair on his forearms, and a cool-looking leather bracelet on his wrist. His hair was very short, and I noticed his sun-kissed face more clearly. Somehow he'd become more handsome than just a few minutes before. It took his holding up a bottle of wine to break my stare.

With the bottle in one hand and a wine glass in the other, he asked, "You a wine girl?" I answered with a grin as I turned, pivoting on one foot like a giddy little school girl.

"White please," I blurted, thinking of my lingering headache and how reds always seemed to aggravate that. I was having a hard time remembering at that moment, but I seemed somewhat satisfied that my answer was on-point.

I strolled from the kitchen into the living room, just as beautiful and tasteful as the kitchen. The living room and dining room were one very large open room, with the sofa separating the room. Behind the sofa stood a sofa table with a pair of Tiffany tulip lamps assigned to each end. The lighting was overall warm and inviting, pink mimosa wafting from the newly lit candles on one of the tables in the living room as well.

I strolled slowly through the living room, stopping to admire a dazzling tapestry on one wall picturing a young blonde ballerina sitting on a white rectangular tufted stool, staring out the window. She wore a black feathered ballerina dress, her face hidden from view.

James whispered into my ear, "Do you like it?" I inhaled sharply. My heart was pounding, and I couldn't move. The warmth of his breath alongside the back of my neck ignited my skin, causing it to tingle. His cologne collected in the back of my nose. I lowered my eyes, glancing to the side he was closest to, and answered while pulling my shoulder up.

"It's amazing."

"Thank you." I knew that he had painted it and my heart leapt, thumping in my chest. "I painted it about five years ago." I swallowed deeply and took the glass, our fingers glancing. I felt my world shift. I looked up from my wine glass to catch his penetrating stare. His worried expression was long gone, replaced by a reassuring smile. I could make out my own reflection in his eyes, and I knew that he felt his world shift too.

It felt as if my knees were going to give way, my lungs struggling to breathe. I couldn't speak, couldn't even find any words not to say. James tilted his glass to mine and whispered, "Cheers."

I looked down at the glass then swiftly back up to meet his

eyes again. "Cheers." We both took our first sip of wine, our eyes locked in that unbroken gaze. The wine was crisp and dry and light, delicious.

James smiled as if he knew how pleased I was and asked, "Do you like it?"

"It's … it's the best I ever had. It's brilliant."

"Glad you like it. We make it here, actually."

"Oh, this is a winery?"

"Three. Like a tour?" He stood back with a slight bow, an inviting open arm to lead me.

We walked past the grand staircase leading to the second floor, when I stopped to more fully appreciate the decor. The space underneath the staircase had been converted into floor-to-ceiling bookcases with an old-fashioned rolling ladder. Framed photos pictured scuba divers in full gear. I focused on a picture of him and a younger lady. "Is that your wife?"

"My daughter." I could only smile at the gentle way in which he answered my question, but he didn't offer any further explanation. I didn't push, but when I saw another picture of another girl, this one only about eight years old, I asked, "Is she yours too?"

"Same girl, years before; Amanda." The light in his eyes dimmed, then he offered, "Haven't seen her in quite a while." I swallowed my wine. I didn't want to ask, but he finally explained, "When my wife got sick a few years ago, Amanda couldn't take it ... and she stayed away. I don't see or hear from her much."

I struggled to find the right words, "I … I'm sorry, James. I have got to learn to keep my big mouth shut!"

"No no, not at all, Elizabeth. I … I'm flattered that you show an interest."

He smiled at me and touched my chin to lift it up to him. I almost wanted to cry. It took everything I had not to hug

16

him.

The bedroom was unbelievably romantic and whimsical and seemed designed for a modern-day princess.

"And *this* room is my favorite."

I gasped. With the wood-beamed ceiling, hand-scraped wood flooring, white-wash gray walls, and the open airy feel of the entire room, all I wanted to do was run and jump on the bed and roll around like a child in a field of daisies. I turned to see the extraordinary stone fireplace which stood gallantly, taking up nearly an entire wall, and had the most amazing white fur rug lying neatly in front of it. A softly lit crystal chandelier hung over the bed, and I could smell the large vanilla candles throughout the room. The bed was made up with a blend of pale blush velvets and shimmery metallic organza, and the mound of pillows plush and alluring.

I ran my fingers across the bedding. "Is this Reilly-Chance?"

He chuckled. "You know your stuff." The warmness of his electric smile ignited the fire within me again. He was seducing me with his eyes and teasing me with his smile.

Turning back toward the front of the house he noted, "I'm out of wine. You?"

I still had half a glass, which I nearly gulped down to hold up an empty glass. "Now that you mention it … "

Heading back to the kitchen, he said, "Time for a little snack too."

# CHAPTER 3
## Breaking Bread

I stood in the kitchen, leaning on the center island, drifting off in thought. I kept going over it in my mind: What an amazing man this James is, how in love he and his wife must have been.

"Elizabeth, do you like seafood?" I shut it off and returned my attention to him. "Yes, I do. And please ... call me *Liz*." He smiled and winked, walking slowly up to me.

"Okay, Liz." My heart jumped faster, harder, butterflies fluttering in my stomach and even through the rest of my body. He was only inches from me then, and getting closer by the second. "How does honey-glazed salmon and a garden fresh salad sound ... Liz?"

"Um," I swallowed. "That sounds delicious ... James."

"Please," he said, "just *Jim*."

Knowing he wanted me to feel at home, I walked over and poured more wine into my glass. He handed me his glass. Our chemistry was undeniable. We were completely at ease with each other.

We lingered in the kitchen, cooking and swaying to the light jazz wafting softly throughout the house. We giggled and laughed with each other, everything felt warm and cozy. There were no awkward silences; our conversations flowed effortlessly. He toured me around the kitchen to the copper pots, the utensils, amidst a lot of heavy gazing and innocent flirting.

Once dinner was on the stove, I wandered around the house a bit more. I didn't want to be rude or nosy, but I did want to know as much about this man, about his life before me, as I could put together without bringing any attention to myself. But I found more pictures of his daughter than himself, which seemed to be perfectly characteristic of such a humble, modest, earthy man.

One of my favorites was a picture of him and his daughter, in a deep embrace on a sandy beach. It was heartwarming to see that moment captured by a photograph. They were tanned bronze, standing in front of an idyllic Caribbean ocean, the smiles across their faces almost as large as the house behind them.

*What a remarkable father he must be*, I couldn't help but think.

But there were absolutely no pictures of his late wife. I couldn't help but wonder why. *Is it too difficult for him to see her face all the time? Was her death too tragic? Is he still in love with her? Is he falling in love with me? Am I as pretty as she was?* My mind became flooded with questions.

Jim stood there, proud and gentlemanly, lighting candles on the table as I stepped into the room. He held out the chair and I slipped in, demure and grateful. He slid me closer to the table, then rested both his hands on my shoulders. His deliberate touch was a welcome surprise. Lifting my hand to touch his, I looked up and said nothing.

He sat to my left. Sitting next to each other was even more intimate than across the table. He lifted his glass. "Here's to a wonderful day with an amazing woman."

My eyes lit up as I raised my own glass to meet his. "Here's to a knight in shining armor."

James nodded and leaned in so closely our glasses slowly met. I could almost hear my inner self begging for him to kiss me. He gazed at me as he leaned in a little bit farther. I wanted to just shove everything off the table and give in to my yearning. He raised my chin slightly and brushed his lips delicately against mine. It was impossible to breathe. My eyes fell shut. Time stood still. My senses heightened as everything around us seemed to vanish. It was just the two of us, alone in a world which existed only for us. It felt like I was in a swirling vortex of sensations as his lips pressed confidently against mine. His sweet cologne, the firmness and warmth of his lips, and the tenderness of his hand touching my chin left me aching for more. He slowly leaned back into his chair as somehow we both took a deep breath and smiled.

The food was delicious, flavorful and colorful, made all the more satisfying to know we'd made it together, and so enjoyed that time. It was more than a meal. It was proof of our match, at least as far as I was already concerned. And I knew he felt the same way, the sexual tension between us was that intense. We sat like civilized people, near strangers, but really we were struggling to simply make it through dinner, and both of us knew it. All I wanted to do was rip his clothes off and make sweet love to this mysterious creation.

Before we knew it, we were laughing out loud about stories he shared about his daughter. I was just grateful for the chance to learn more about him, the strange circumstances of my own presence there went entirely unnoticed.

We were laughing so hard that somehow my hair came undone, and began to slowly fall down around my face. I pulled it back up when he reached out for my hand. "Please … don't … " His eyes softened. He gently touched my hair, tracing the waves around my face and whispered, "My god." Jim continued, "You are the most beautiful thing I have ever seen." I became acutely aware of the vulnerability in his eyes, his sincerity. The deeper I looked the more mesmerized I became. It was as if he had penetrated my soul.

Layla walked up beside us. She whimpered and nudged

his leg with her head that broke the spell we both seemed to be under. Jim cleared his throat. "Hey, girl. You need to go out?" She smiled as she wagged her tail. Jim excused himself to let her out while I went to freshen up.

A few moments later, the happy dog accompanied Jim back to the kitchen where he stoked the fire and I grabbed another bottle of wine. I couldn't remember if we were on the second or the third bottle, and it didn't seem to matter. I was starting to feel all that liquid courage. My head began to ache and throb, and so did other parts of my body.

We sat back down, our chairs touching. He leaned over to take my hand and traced the outline of my fingers. "Where did you get this?" I looked down to a small scar across the top of my hand. "Oh that's … " I began to say. "It's from … well, I guess I don't remember right now."

It was starting to get warm with the fire fully ablaze. I offered to do the dishes. He seemed a bit disappointed, but smiled and graciously accepted. Really, I just needed a little time to think and breathe and figure out what was going on, what had happened, and what was about to happen.

The chemistry between us, the raw animal magnetism, was intoxicating. Not only was he drop-dead gorgeous, he was gentle in nature, funny, and extremely talented, a man of kindness and compassion. It was so easy to talk with him. We both seemed to laugh at each other's jokes, no matter how corny they may have been. I was completely amazed and excited, stunned and thrilled, and extremely sexually frustrated at this point.

After the table was cleared, I took my purse and slipped away to try and collect myself in the bathroom again, maybe find an extra toothbrush and some toothpaste somewhere.

I turned right to go into the bathroom and saw the door directly across the hallway, one of two rooms he'd ignored on our tour. *Is it a guest bedroom,* I wondered, *or an office?* The more I wondered, the more I realized how little I knew of the man, and how quickly I was to ignore that fact, and how dangerous that could still be.

# CHAPTER 4
## Lizzie Takes a Bow

I stood at the bathroom sink reliving what had happened over these last few hours. I pulled the lipstick from my purse, staring back at the reflection in the mirror. A wave of tantalizing seduction flowed through me. Patience was receding, passion taking over. I wanted to take my time, not throw myself at him, to learn more, to anticipate, to play hard to get.

But it wasn't going to be easy.

My inner self had grown stronger over the years, and she wanted what she wanted. I'd come to think of her as *Lizzie*. Liz was generally soft-spoken and polite. But Lizzie was the wild child. Lizzie was Liz's other, hungrier, sexier self, her id run wild. And what Lizzie wanted, Lizzie got.

Liz may have shuffled down the hall of St. Mary's Catholic School for Girls, but Lizzie liked to strut, shirt tied in a knot under her burgeoning breasts, tanned thighs above her tight white knee socks.

And in that bathroom, I could see Lizzie staring out at me from the other side of that mirror.

Lizzie wanted out. Lizzie wanted Jim.

That's when the strains of the acoustic guitar strumming leaked in through the door, coaxing me back out.

I thought I'd find Jim sitting in the kitchen or the living room, but he was nowhere in sight. But that guitar got slightly louder as I followed it through the house. It seemed to be coming from the porch on the far side of the living room. It got louder, clearer as I walked closer.

The back door was slightly ajar, so I opened it and stepped out onto the back porch. I felt like I'd stepped into an Italian enchanted garden. I recognized the very large potted olive trees on either side of the back door as I walked out onto a cobblestone patio. It was quite spectacular. Jim was sitting on the edge of a large corner sectional facing a huge patio fireplace. A new fire was just barely flickering. He sat playing, his back to me, but stopped as he heard me approach.

"Please," I said softly, "don't stop. It's … it's lovely."

I was whisked away in the fairytale atmosphere, the cool breeze against the backs of my naked legs. The leaves of a large olive tree, rising up from the middle of the patio which had been built around it, seemed to hum a melody of tranquility as the cool breeze flowed through them. It was unusually beautiful and groomed to absolute perfection.

As I got closer to the tree I could see a large heart-shaped etching in its bark, and inside the heart were the letters, *J. D. + B. A.* Instead of being jealous or distracted, I was reassured. This truly was the sweet-souled man I'd taken him to be.

I wondered, *Maybe this tree was where they met and fell in love. Do I remind him of his lost love, and maybe that's why he invited me into his home? What a gift for the both of them. The kind of love most people only dream of.*

But soon enough it was Lizzie's voice in my head, not my own. *Quit your whining,* she said to me in the back of my brain, *and go talk to him!* I closed my eyes to listen to the guitar, taking a deep breath, enjoying an easy smile. I opened my eyes to see him tentatively watching over me, so I drifted over and sat down on the sofa next to him.

But I could feel myself getting tired. I was so at ease and relaxed that I didn't even second-guess the idea of lying on the couch next to him. I stared up at the stars, music in the distance. I was snuggled in the moment, in love with the moment, wishing it would never end. But I knew it would, eventually. It would have to. The best I could do was close my eyes and lie back and enjoy it while I could.

.

# CHAPTER 5
## The Day of All Days

"Good morning, sunshine." I opened my eyes from the bed to see the door cracked, Jim peeking his head in. I rubbed my eyes and looked around, confusion fading fast as I took in the sumptuous bedding around me. I sat straight up in the bed, threw my blonde hair back over my head, and pulled the blankets up over my chest.

I hoarsely answered while clearing my throat, "Good morning, Jim."

"How are you feeling?" he asked, holding out a cup of coffee for me, as though asking permission to enter.

"Oh, fine … I think. Wow, so I guess I must have fallen asleep. I'm so sorry."

"No reason to be. I thought you'd be more comfortable sleeping in here as opposed to on the back porch. I hope you don't mind. I didn't see that you had a change of clothes, so I found some old things of Beth Ann's. Since you two are practically the same size, I brought some things in for you to see if there is anything you might like to wear." He pointed toward the closet and then to another door. "The guest bath is right through that door, so make yourself at home."

I took a taste of my freshly brewed coffee, and could faintly smell the aroma of breakfast lingering through the doorway.

"Hope you're hungry!"

I laughed, returning the witty comment with, "Hope it's as good as it smells!" I could hear his muffled laughter as he closed the bedroom door on his way out.

I showered, towel-dried my hair and threw it back up. I also found extra toothbrushes and a tube of toothpaste, which I assumed he kept on-hand for his daughter when she came to visit. I caught myself moving my head to the beat and humming to Elton John's "Bennie and the Jets" playing through the wall. I finished getting cleaned up and walked into the kitchen where Jim was putting the final touches on breakfast.

Jim turned from the range to serve up bacon and scrambled eggs, fresh from the skillet. A basket of freshly baked croissants sat on the table.

"Wow, you made these?"

"Well, not me personally. Beth Ann owned a bakery in downtown San Merhita. It was doing so well I decided to keep it, because one can never go wrong when fresh bread and chocolate cake are at your beck and call," he continued in a quiet laugher. It was as if he were trying to comfort himself by chuckling through the words. But the smile didn't last.

We sat down and Jim smiled comfortably, seeming relaxed, at home in a pair of jeans and a black Steely Dan t-shirt. The bountiful breakfast was almost as fulfilling as merely being in the same room with him. I enjoyed each bite, the peppery bacon, the farm-fresh eggs, those fluffy rolls. Nothing had ever tasted better. The morning light shined soft through the shutters, casting Jim in a handsome glow. But I caught myself staring and looked way.

During the meal I would catch his glance, he would catch mine, and we would both look back down at our food trying to disguise our smiles. It was so innocent and pure. I never thought I'd still be able to have such feelings at my age. In my forties, I wasn't a kid anymore. These kinds of things didn't happen to women in my stage of life.

At least that's what I'd thought.

"So, I don't mean to intrude," I said even as I once again prepared to intrude, "but … I saw initials on the tree, *J. D. + B.A.* I get that *B. A.* stands for Beth Ann, and the *J*, that's *Jim*, right? So, what's the *D*?"

"*Dean*. I didn't have a middle name, so … "

I didn't have to think about it for long. "Wait a minute … your name is *James Dean*?"

He nodded with a casual smile. "No relation."

When we had nearly cleared our plates, Jim's mood began to shift. He seemed almost tense. I placed my napkin in my lap. "Everything all right? Are you sure it's okay that I'm here?"

Setting his hand on mine, he said, "It's absolutely okay that you're here." He leaned back in his chair. "In fact, if you don't have any place you have to be today, I'd love to show you around. Maybe take you for a ride? I have some things I need to do today, and I would love the company." His look was that of a boy asking a girl if she'd like to spend the day with him. I couldn't resist.

"I don't have anywhere I need to be today," I said, trying to be casual.

Jim stood up from his chair. "I'll clean up here if you'd like to change into something a little more casual," he excitedly coaxed. "There are plenty of clothes in the closet in your room. Might want to bring a sweater. Oh, and I'm not sure if the boots will fit you; but if they do, throw them on."

I changed into some jeans to match the royal blue shirt I had on. I draped a pretty slate gray sweater over my shoulders. I looked around, but Jim wasn't in the kitchen. Then I heard a car horn coming from the front. I opened the door and saw him sitting in the hottest silver '55 Porsche 356 Speedster convertible I had ever seen. He jumped out and ran over to the passenger side, opening the door for me. "Your chariot awaits, madam."

We drove down the same gravel road which brought us in, but this time I took a more conscientious look at the grandeur of his property. The autumn-colored vineyards wound up and down the hills. A very large building stood about a half mile on the other side of the house. "What is that building over there?"

"That's the winery. There's a separate entrance way over there. I can take you by, if you'd like."

"Sounds great." We drove past that familiar infamous green sign which read, *San Francisco 54 miles south, San Merhita 7 miles north*. "Jim, which way are we going?"

"Left for just a few miles. There's a park on the cliffside I'd like to take you, then we can go into San Merhita for a little while."

"Whatever you'd like," I said. "You're driving, after all."

He peeled out onto the two-lane highway as if to give me a taste of just what his beautiful toy could do. A little startled by the speed, I reached over to grab his hand resting on the gear shift. He chuckled as he slowly seated his sunglasses on the bridge of his nose. I couldn't help but stare at him. He was so handsome. It was hard to keep my eyes on anything else.

The warm sun on my face and the breeze on my arms was so warm and inviting. I threw my head back on my headrest, closed my eyes, pulled my arms up over my head, and let out a girlish squeal, "*Yyyyyowwww!*" He busted out into an uncontrollable laughter. Time stood still as I looked over and saw the smile on his face.

*Beth Ann was such a lucky lady,* I thought. I couldn't tell if it was the smell of the antique car leather, the salt in the air, or the mixture of both, but I couldn't seem to keep my thoughts from swirling round and round in my head, thinking, *What a wonderful life this must have been for her.*

The salt in the air became the more prominent fragrance as we turned onto a gravel road. Seagulls circled overhead, eager to share their natural bounty. We followed a slight incline which ended at the most stunning and massive rock cliffside outcropping I had ever seen.

The cliffside protruded at the lip, overlooking the churning Pacific Ocean. It was all absolutely spectacular.

I looked down to see the waves crashing into the rocky beachside, enjoying the sounds of the ocean and the calling of the seagulls. The air seemed different somehow. It was so pure, and seemed to cleanse my entire body. The breeze pushed my hair across my face then back with the shifting winds. Looking out over that cliff, I was struck with a feeling of the oddly familiar. I didn't have any clear, concise memory of the place, but I felt certain that I'd been there before, and more than once.

But on at least one occasion, that was a place of great importance to me, almost magical significance. I took a deep breath and closed my eyes, searching for my memories. When I couldn't find them, the beauty of the surroundings faded behind a cold chill running up my spine.

*When was I here before?* I silently pleaded with my secretive, smarter self. *Was it ... a wedding?*

Visions of wedding veils and a small chamber quartet, black tuxedos and light blue dresses, champagne and a cool breeze, the churning of the waves beneath.

*That's it,* I tried to convince myself. *It must be. Was it Jim's wedding? Yes, that's it! Jim's wedding ... to Beth Ann, it has to be. Did I know Jim before all this, before my recent episode? It must be! No wonder he's so friendly to me, so helpful. He's a friend!*

I searched through that phasing fog inside my head. *But how did we come to know each other? And why am I here with him now, and not home with my own husband?*

*Where is my husband?* I had to ask myself, a sudden dizzying feeling making me feel like I was going to fall over the lip of the cliff, crashing to the rocks below. *Why aren't I with him now? What was I doing yesterday when I passed out, where was I going ... and why?*

I had to let it go for the time being. With a sigh and a nod, I glanced around again and tried to put the rest of it out of my mind. "It's gorgeous, really, just beautiful."

He said, "It is when *you're* here."

Jim pulled me close, gently placing both hands on the back of my neck, stroking my right cheek bone with his thumb. I felt the sweet pressure of his lips on mine. I could barely keep my balance as he began stroking my hair as his tongue teasingly caressed the inside of my lip. My feet left the ground as he effortlessly scooped me up, cradling me in both his arms. He was so much stronger than I realized. I caressed his cheeks with my hands as he carried me toward the car. Jim gently leaned over, seating me on the top of my headrest. His hand traced the outline of my chin, he rested his forehead on mine. "You taste so good. But we can't stay."

He walked around to his side and I slid down into my seat. Jim just smiled as he started the car and slowly followed the gravel road back down the hill. I turned to watch the majestic view recede behind us.

We drove for just a few miles through the rolling vineyard hills and into San Merhita. The little Old Spanish town was buzzing with activity. We passed a couple of small art galleries, a beautiful Spanish mission. The local farmers' market was in full swing, the streets filled with people hocking their wares. The vibrant colors of the different fruits and vegetables were inviting and bountiful. We drove past a small crowd of adults and children surrounding a local saxophone player on the corner of the village. There were multitudes of bouquets of mixed flowers and peonies for sale, the sweet aroma of freshly baked bread getting stronger as we pulled into a parking place by a sidewalk full of wrought iron tables and chairs. A few folks turned to offer a friendly wave as Jim invited me in.

"Oh," I surmised. "This is your bakery. Yes, yes, I'd love to see it." It was bustling with people. Baskets of homemade artisan wood-fired breads, handcrafted pastries, homemade jams and jellies, and the smell of cinnamon citrus sugar in the air decorated the bakery. It was heaven.

I pointed to one intriguingly named pastry. Jim explained, "Oh, that's our cherry cheesecake strudel. It's plaited croissant dough with a cheesecake and sour cherry filling, and of course the cherry topping. It's quite delicious. Let's bring a few home for later."

He raised an arm to grab the attention of one of the workers, who eagerly made his way over to us. "Hey, Jim!" They shook hands.

"Running this place into rack and ruin I see, Philip!" The two men shared a hearty laugh as he redirected the introduction over to me. "Liz, shop's manager, Phillip Gaven." He turned to his underling. "Phillip, this is Liz."

I reached out my hand to shake his when he gently kissed my hand, in a very gentlemanly fashion. "What can I do for you folks today, sir?" Philip asked. Jim pointed to the cherry cheesecake strudel and said, "Two to go."

"Yes, sir, right away. And may I say, sir, we're all very excited about tonight."

"Phillip, please, stop with the yes sir, no sir stuff."

"Sorry … Jim."

We took our pastries, shared a few more pleasantries, then headed to Jim's car. I asked him, "What's going on this evening?" He smiled at me, intriguing, secretive. Liz didn't love it, but Lizzie was certainly intrigued.

"Annual gathering. Care to attend?"

"Well, I … I wouldn't want to impose."

"Then I'll insist."

I slid back into the car and he closed the door.

He took me for a brief tour of the rest of the small Spanish town. While I watched him point here and there and saw his lips move, speaking about the various points of interest of the town, I couldn't hear a word he was saying. All I could do was stare at him and wonder, *Where did he come from? Was there ever a man this graciously and effortlessly gorgeous?*

He leaned over and touched my hand. "We'll head to the house, but there is someplace else I'd like to take you."

"Um, somewhere else?" I couldn't deny a sense of tiredness coming over me, which I chalked up to the accident the day before. But I was so enjoying my time with Jim, I just couldn't refuse.

We headed back to the area I soon recognized as his property entrance, but we passed the turn. I turned and pointed. "Jim, I think we missed your turn."

"I have a couple things I have to do at the winery. Shouldn't take long." Before I had a chance to say anything, we turned into this immaculately landscaped, sweeping vineyard with a large sign which read, *Stone Canyon Vineyards*. A very long driveway led us up to a huge parking lot bustling with cars. It looked like there was a bridal party under a big oak tree about twenty yards to my right. We entered a gate marked *Employees* and drove to the back of a large red barn. The stone foundation alone rose feet above the ground. This was no boutique winery, but a huge distillery.

The grounds were complete with an old-fashioned wine store, grapevines adorning the entire front of the building. We drove around to the back of this big beautiful barn and he parked the car. "I won't be long."

I leaned back in my seat a bit and closed my eyes to soak in the warm sun, as though it were kissing my face.

I must have dozed off while Jim was inside, because it startled me when he walked up to me, touched my arm. "Sorry it took so long. Let's get you back to the house."

A slight chill ran through the air, so I put on the sweater I'd brought. Jim raised the convertible top and rolled up the windows. The beautiful reddish orange of the sky was stunning as the sun began its descent over the mountains.

# CHAPTER 6
## The Gathering

We walked through the back door and into the kitchen. I set the bakery box on the island while Jim grabbed a couple of wine glasses. He pulled a bottle from the wine fridge. He poured us both a glass, then toasted, "To a beautiful day," as our glasses clinked. "And to a wonderful evening … and a beautiful night."

With that, Jim took my hand and led me to the guest bedroom. I turned on the lamp as I entered to find a gorgeous long, black, sequined, evening gown laying on the bed. I walked farther into the bedroom and saw Jim wink with a smile as he closed the door behind me. I gasped at the stunning sequins, and gently traced its outline.

There was a white piece of paper on the black dress, which read, *I will always remember how wonderful you will look tonight. With much love, Jim.* I shrieked with excitement. I grabbed the dress, threw it in front of me and ran over to the mirror to see how I might look with it on.

I turned on the stereo next to the bed and found some beautiful blues, Billie Holiday, grand and sweeping. I swayed to the music as I sipped a little more wine. I floated around the room and practically waltzed into the bathroom to start the shower.

*Uh-oh,* I warned myself, *too much wine. This is Liz's night, not Lizzie's!*

I undressed and stepped into the hot shower. The day's salty ocean air clung to my skin, my hair, but was soon blasted away by that steamy water, the thick and soapy suds smooth against my skin. I tried not to recall how amazing it felt when Jim cradled my face in his hands, how his kiss sent shockwaves through my body, as his fingers ran through my hair during our embrace. When my thoughts shifted from our kiss to how magnificent a lover Jim would be, it was obvious Lizzie was enjoying him every bit as much as I was.

I couldn't help imagining Jim opening the shower door to ravage me right there. *Oh, Lizzie would love that*, I knew.

His sultry look was fixated, as though he were spellbound. Lizzie smiled slightly when she realized he entered the shower behind her, but she never acknowledged him. He stepped behind her, slowly began massaging her back with the hot soapy water. Her back remained facing him, hot water sliding down her neck, long wet hair draped. She stood there, wanting … waiting. Lizzie pulled her hair over to one side, as though inviting him to come closer.

Lizzie felt Jim cup her breasts in his hands, and felt his warm hairy front against her smooth backside. She knew he couldn't contain his excitement as he pressed hard against her. She felt his hand slowly reach down to tease her left nipple as he inched his hand up to her mouth, keeping his finger on her mouth to keep her silent. His taking control was a dangerous turn-on for Lizzie. Any man who could contain her would be a force to reckon with. She braced herself with her hands on either side of the shower walls as he took his left hand to pull back her wet hair, twisting it as though to pull. Leaning over her, he maneuvered his hand over her leg, through the heat of her soapy wetness. Jim massaged her inviting entry with the texture of his fingers.

Lizzie smiled as she closed her eyes in moaning delight. His tongue on her ear, the heat of his breath, the strength of his hand over her mouth, and the penetration of his finger inside her was becoming too much, even for her. He continued the in-and-out motion of his finger. Lizzie slowly moved her hand over his, guiding his rhythm, and the two of them began pleasuring her together. It was all about her, and both of them knew it. Their interlocking cadence shook Lizzie to her very core and her breathing became heavy and strained.

She guided him faster, as he sucked on her neck. She let out a moan of extreme satisfaction as he brought her to the moment she had been fantasizing about. She turned to face Jim, because she was only getting started. She sat down on the shower seat, opening her knees to him, while using her finger to motion him in. Jim eagerly obeyed as though pleasuring Lizzie was his primary function, his only reason for being. He knelt and Lizzie pulled his hands to her thighs. His right hand traced the curvature of her leg, as his left hand began to circle the inside of her thigh. He taunted Lizzie with his mouth, as though he knew precisely what she longed for. Her fingers ran over his head, and she pulled his mouth to her wetness. Jim kissed her wetness gently, then probed his tongue in and out teasingly, just to get a taste. Lizzie thrust her head back in anticipation. Jim slowly stood up and kissed Lizzie firmly on her mouth.

"No," he said, "not yet."

Lizzie looked up at him, wide-eyed and begging. He pulled her chin up to his while whispering, "This is just a taste. I want you to be ready for tonight."

Lizzie had met her match. She closed her eyes to absorb the tingling throughout her body. When she opened her eyes Jim was gone. Yet, she questioned this, as she didn't hear the shower door open or close.

I looked around the shower, alone. *Just a daydream,* I told myself*, just getting carried away. At least … I hope that was all it was!*

I dried off and stepped out of the shower to see the fireplace was fully stoked and burning. Was it ever! I wrapped the towel around my soaked hair, wrapped another towel around my body, and walked into the bedroom to find he had laid out a beautiful set of jewelry and a black/gold masquerade mask. I picked up the mask and walked out of the bedroom.

"Jim?" I called. "James?"

I walked down the hall to what I knew was his master bedroom. I knocked.

"Yes?"

I cleared my throat. "Um, Jim … "

After my lingering pause, he answered, "Yes, Liz?"

"Jim, what kind of gathering is this going to be tonight … precisely?"

He opened the door with only a towel covering his lower half. He smiled when he saw me in nothing but towels. "Well hello, lovely." I shook my head to re-ask the question, holding up the mask.

Jim chuckled. "It's just an annual ball I host. The masks give the guests a sense of anonymity." Satisfied with his answer, I returned back to my room.

Feeling a little ashamed and embarrassed, I began to apply my makeup and fix my hair, though neither could compare to the diamond necklace and earrings he left me. I slipped into the backless, black, sequined gown, dipping so low that no undergarment could be worn.

I didn't feel like Lizzie would miss it. I put the finishing touches on my makeup and began to apply our lipstick choice. I would have actually considered a soft pink lip, but Lizzie preferred deep red.

Lizzie finished with the last of the curls on the half-up hairstyle she decided on. She set the evening off with a final sweep of rose lipstick, as she puckered and winked into the mirror, then turned to exit the bathroom.

Lizzie made her way into the living room where she heard music in the distance. It was coming from outside. She held her mask in her left hand, nearly empty glass of wine in the other, and slowly made her way out the door to the large back porch.

Chinese lanterns hung everywhere. It seemed every branch of every tree had a twinkling Chinese lantern hanging from it. The only other light was from the full moon breaking through the clouds. The lanterns dimly led the path through a dense forest. The open breeze was cool and gentle, music wafting from that darkened glen.

Two guards stood at the entrance, both in black-caped tuxedos and blank white plastic masks. They saw me walking toward them, and they immediately pulled back the tree-stemmed entrance to motion my welcome. I was offered to exchange my empty wine glass for a glass of champagne, which I gladly did. I tasted one mouth-watering drop of the enticing nectar and found myself only looking for one person.

I looked around, wondering, *Where's Jim?*

This area was enormous, unlike anything I had ever seen before. Inside the area, it was lit exquisitely by candlelight. The music which allured me to the area wasn't the same once I entered. All of a sudden it changed. Everything changed.

# CHAPTER 7
## The Rose

I walked through an entrance of enchantment and delight, Lizzie's primal playground. A tall, muscular man approached me, wearing a black tuxedo and cloak, with a very knightly mask covering his strong, chiseled features. I took another sip of champagne. The more I drank, the more I wanted, the more effective it was. The outline of his face and his thick, dark brown hair suggested a handsome face behind the mask. I tried to speak but he brushed his gloved finger up to his mouth as if to halt me from speaking.

Lizzie was in heaven.

I felt like I'd walked into the untouchable workings of my inner mind come to life. In looking back, I now know I was being thrown into a maze of the epitome, or embodiment, of the most pivotal sexual encounters I had ever experienced, or would ever experience. The greeter draped my hand through the bend of his arm.

I walked slowly alongside him, wondering what lay ahead of me, absorbing every second of every moment. A slight muffled chanting sound got louder as we passed one room after another, only drapes securing the privacy of whomever was inside, whatever they were doing.

A fog drifted along the floor at my feet. My escort caressed my hand, and I felt a warm presence behind me. Two escorts towered on either side behind me, yet I didn't feel I was in any danger. *Mea Culpa* played in the background. My escort led me to a large velvet-lined room. I knew something special was going to happen, something I'd be witnessing or be a part of, but nothing I could ignore or escape.

I was still not wearing my mask, idle in my hand. Drinking the champagne was participation enough for me at that point.

*Where the hell is Jim?*

Breathless chanting surrounded me as I stepped inside the velvet-lined room, excitement in the air. Men and women, all in mysterious robes and capes and masks, faced in a single direction, but they were blocking my view. Whatever held their attention, I couldn't see it.

But Lizzie insisted.

The seductive fragrance of candles lingered in the air, and the powerful sound of the Benedictine music seemed to vibrate throughout my body. The velvet curtains were luxurious, the gloved hand on my arm seemed strangely erotic to me. A slight tingle passed through my entire body. It was a shared sensation, a communal energy. Everyone there shared the same bond, and the euphoria we were unchaining would be nothing short of epic. I had one thing on my mind at this point, and that was my desire to share this rush of exhilaration and contentment with Jim.

Everybody was looking around. *Who are they looking for? What's going to happen here?*

*Must be Jim,* I guessed. But everybody's attention kept turning to me, a shiver running up my spine. I tried to ignore it, but every mask turned to me, little steps bringing them all closer.

*Wait,* I wondered, *are they waiting ... for me?*

A large wooden table was covered with deep red rose petals. On either side of the table sat flickering candelabras, and in the center lay a perfectly shaped woman with long dark hair, a black-feathered mask covering only her eyes, and she held a bright red rose in one hand and a glass of champagne in the other.

And nothing else.

I quickly came to think of her as *Rose*, jet black stiletto heels and nothing else. She sipped her champagne as she began intently studying my every move. She seemed to purr with excitement. She motioned me toward her, then placed her finger to her face, tracing the outline of her red lips. I felt the sudden warmth of her obvious desire for me.

To intensify Rose's anticipation, I slowed my pace even more. I wanted to tease her. Tasting my champagne, I resumed my approach. Her lips parted, and she smirked upon realizing how boldly I had decided to participate. Her eyes widened from the thrill, and her lustful gaze smoldered as the erection of her nipples proved obvious. I paused a few feet away from the table, waiting for her next move. Her breathing deepened. She licked her lower lip as she nibbled it ever so slightly. The music became louder, more intense, the crowd's attention even more keenly fixed upon us. I took those final few steps toward her. The candlelight dimmed, with only a few sparkling lights remaining.

Rose came to her knees on this bed adorned with roses and signaled for my escorts to assist. One positioned himself behind me, and began kissing my neck as he unzipped my dress. The other assisted him by pulling my dress away while nuzzling my ear. My original escort knelt down to help me up to the table. He looked up to me, as if begging my approval. I nodded, prompting his relieving moan. He sounded desperate to be permitted to taste all that awaited him. His eyes were fixed on mine, as if his gratification was solely based on my expressive communication of his role. He began probing my thighs with his mouth and tongue, as the guards began kissing my neck and caressing the plumpness of my breasts. I stood there waiting for more. My breathing became heavy, the wetness of his tongue began to travel further up my thigh. Rose reached for me as her finger lightly brushed my firm nipple. I looked up at her and our eyes became transfixed.

It was such an overwhelming sensation of awareness, being passionately kissed and exhilaratingly handled by two lovers at once. And the endless line of applicants fervently waiting to please, even more than the previous participant, left me aching to test them. It was dangerously erotic and intoxicatingly enticing. I looked around once more for Jim, but he was nowhere to be found. Rose reached for me again. Her eyes were tantalizing, pleading. Her body yearned for mine. Liz was trepidatious, but Lizzie was leaping up and down with capricious excitement, and her lustful throbbing would soon overpower my other concerns.

The rushing desire to let go and be deliciously pleasured by so many at once was beyond my comprehension. Around me, the others were kissing and sensually fondling each other. They were anxiously watching me and Rose. I smiled, knowing I was the one who was quenching their thirst, slaking their hunger. With baited breath, they awaited to continue their own gratification. Their motions were fluid and precise. The glorious melody of seductive sighs and orgasmic moans elated me. I was ready.

Rose motioned the guards to carry me to the table. She intently watched me, circling the bed with her black tassel she held firmly in her hand. Rose rounded the table to position herself at my head, as she looked down into my eyes. Leaning over to kiss my abdomen, Rose grazed her breast on my lips. She pulled back then bent over to gently open my lips while she dripped champagne into my mouth. I swallowed, licked my lips, and motioned for more. Rose trickled champagne over my breasts, as she giggled with delight. My nipples were plump and pink as the blood rushed to fill them. They were fully attentive and completely erect from the cold champagne. The excitement of the tassel made me breathe harder. I lay still on my back. My thigh-highs and heels were still on, but nothing else. Rose smiled with approval as she walked back around to the foot of the table. She brought more champagne, and I was holding my mouth open, practically begging for more. Lizzie was definitely begging for more.

One of the guards approached with a very long red scarf. He draped it over my eyes, tying it underneath the table, so as to restrain my head while covering my eyes. My breathing became quick and shallow. I could hear the quiet chanting and the music in the background as the excitement built. I felt my wrists tenderly being tied to the sides with a scarf-like material. I felt her warm tongue on mine as she teased me incessantly. I could feel the heat of her breath on my ear as she very quietly whispered, "*Shhhhhhhhh.*" I tasted champagne on my lips. But when I opened my mouth for more I received, instead the softness of her thigh against my tongue, her thighs rubbing against the soft lobes of my ears. She seemed to hover above me, her legs giving me room to move beneath her. She knew exactly what she wanted, and she wasted no time coaching me. I slowly moved the tip of my tongue in and out through my lips, providing the generous rhythm she obviously craved. Rose groaned with liberated excitement when she could hear the sweet sound of her nectar ballet through my lips. I started to circle my tongue to finally taste her essence, when I felt several hands on my legs, and my knees being slightly pulled apart. The fresh sensation of a firm, wet tongue probing the inside of my thigh was unbelievably erotic. A soft hand massaged one of my breasts, plucking my nipple, supple lips explored my other nipple.

I turned my attention to the throngs of worshippers around me. At that point, I didn't know or care who was participating. The music echoed and the moaning of other men and women challenging each other rose up to underscore it in orgasmic counterpoint. Nothing had ever felt so natural. Full, raw, animal magnetism boldly captured me. I became dissociated from everything but this intoxicating sensation of physical exaltation, of rapturous delight.

Rose's ride began to heighten. Her juices started to flow, as her movements became seemingly uncontrollable. Her lips began to swell as she neared her intention.

More champagne came, I didn't even know from where or from whom, but I lapped it up. The hot breath of somebody's mouth made its way down my stomach. I shifted, making sure that mouth wound up right where I wanted it. My breathing deepened. Rose moaned in response.

Rose bucked wildly, heat rising up from between her thighs. The others wailed with euphoria. I could taste her nearness, which only made me want to tease her more. The final flick of my tongue sent Rose over the edge. Her hips began to thrust as she lay back. Her heavy moans intensified. She soon became lifeless as she dismounted. Her mouth soon covered mine, as she shared in her flavor. Her kiss more obsessive and appreciative than before.

She offered more champagne. I kept partaking in every way possible, as I could feel all eyes attentively on me. Tongues lapped up all over my body and I no longer cared who or what, the sinful euphoria of the thought alone was enough to make me orgasm incessantly. Somebody slipped their tongue into my pussy. This combination became all-consuming. The wet sucking sounds and pulsating tongues opened the door to a brand new glorious dimension for me. Soon, my feet were unbound, then my arms. I found myself fully engaged in the most passionate kisses imaginable. We were as one in mind, body, and soul. I thought, *This has to be*

*Jim.* But once my hands were free to move about, my hands ran through a head full of long hair.

It was Rose, and she and I were drinking the same champagne. She kissed me passionately, feeding me champagne in between kisses, but the hot breaths and tongues I was feeling everywhere else were coming from different directions. The stimulating warmth of my wetness traveled up my body. I ached and my world spun wildly with the flickering tease of multiple wet tongues. I enjoyed every forbidden moment of it, moaning in a voice I barely recognized. Sweat rolled down my body. Their bodies moved in sync with mine, moans getting louder. My heart pounded as I gasped for breath. My vision blurred. I quivered at the peak of explosion. The rush of adrenaline pulsated my extremities as I came.

In an attempt to recover, I removed my scarf and moved from the bed to a very large throne-like chair draped in velvet. I inhaled deeply and sat upright, positioning my left leg over the left arm of the chair, and my right leg over the other. Rose placed herself in a chair facing me on the opposite side of the room. I continued my gaze to acknowledge the rest of my applicants. They waited for my nod. I kept them waiting. Still attempting to recover from my out-of-body experience, I sat, sipping champagne, while allowing them to indulge and quench their thirst.

Each one knelt before me to express their appreciation with their tongue, I ran my fingers through their hair.

Rose watched me greet my adoring throngs, and I enjoyed her viewing, each playing her part in a mutual game that only got more intense as the moments went on, no words spoken, no skin touching, an entire room between us.

Hours must have passed. I wanted to satisfy those around me as much as they were pleasuring me, but it wasn't about them. This was completely about me and no one else but me. Their fulfillment was solely based on my satisfaction.

Lizzie wasn't finished being in control. She reached for her mask laying right beside her and pulled it up to her face, placing it over her sultry eyes.

Everything changed. Quietness blanketed the bellowing moans of the others.

Lizzie stood up and suddenly found herself in her favorite pose, a position of supreme power. All eyes were transfixed on Lizzie, anticipating, awaiting her instructions. Lizzie pointed to Rose. Rose immediately stood up. Lizzie pointed to the table and Rose submitted. She lay on her back on the table, running her hands down her own smooth bronzed body, arching her back in expectation. Lizzie summoned several men and women to stand around and worship Rose's loveliness.

Rose repositioned herself so that she was on all fours atop the table. Lizzie understood the indirect request and granted Rose's wish. Taking charge of the situation, Lizzie studiously walked through the crowd of spectators, scanning for the one applicant she felt could offer Rose the most pleasure. She summoned a towering, dark-skinned man. He stood confidently, shoulders back, spine erect, a massive bulge under his robe. Lizzie stood squarely in front of him, looking him over from top to bottom. She leaned in and lusciously kissed him on the lips. He was *the chosen one*. This strapping young lad was very eager and willing to please, and it showed in his smile. Lizzie's eyes widened as she smiled.

Lizzie and her chosen one walked to Rose, as Rose began whipping her long dark hair over to one side. Rose licked and nibbled on her lower lip as Lizzie returned to the table beside her. Lizzie retrieved the tassel from Rose's grip and began to repeatedly stroke it through her hand. Lizzie smoothly grazed her fingers across the chosen one's firm buttocks as she turned him around to face her. Lizzie's eyes met his as she leaned down to pull his nipple to her mouth. His breathing became labored as she dropped to a squat. Their eyes remained locked as she mischievously slid his rock hard manhood into the fiery moistness of her mouth. Lizzie's eyes pierced deeply into his soul as she pulled him in deeply. His hands cupped Lizzie's head as she rocked back and forth. He exhaled forcefully as she continued. Lizzie finished by licking and moistening him just enough to redirect his interest to Rose. Lizzie stood up long enough to stroke his lips with her tongue and gently whisk the tassel across the smooth of his buttocks as he tugged his hardness.

Lizzie strutted to the head of the table as she stroked Rose's back with the feathered tassel. Rose smirked at her selfishly until Lizzie finally returned, dominant over her, defying her look. With his rod behind her and Lizzie in front, Rose was subjugated to their whim. Lizzie dared Rose to interfere in her gaze. Lizzie gazed forbiddingly and intently into Rose's eyes. What Lizzie wanted most was to watch Rose's expression when the chosen one stuck that massive manhood into her.

And whatever Lizzie wanted, Lizzie got.

The chosen one circled Rose's buttocks with the palm of his hand then bent over to delectably moisten her entry with his tongue. Rose's eyes and head rolled back as she let out a long and low moan. He primed his stiffness and began his entrance. Lizzie forcefully pulled Rose's chin up so she could gaze soulfully into her eyes. One thrust and Rose's pupils quickly sharpened as she gasped from the initial bolt shooting uncontrollably through her body. Lizzie's eyes widened with excitement. The chosen one pulled Rose's hips closer for another driving bore. Rose winced and let out a slight cry, looking deeply into Lizzie's eyes. Lizzie's thumb brushed the fullness of Rose's lips, but she demanded Rose not break her gaze. Rose moaned for more. Lizzie raised her hand to her side and flogged the tassel around the chosen one's buttocks. He raised a growling moan as he drew Rose's hips into him. Rose became more unquenchable, and she began to whimper and whine for more. Another forceful thrust and Rose cried out. The sting of his thrust caught her. His motion increased. Lizzie groaned in complete delight from inflicting Rose's throbbing pleasure. Lizzie caressed Rose's face as she whipped the tassel across his buttocks again, commanding more. Rose kept groaning as she gazed into Lizzie's eyes, a stare of absolute satisfaction and mutual understanding.

But Lizzie wasn't quite finished.

The chosen one kept a steady pace. Tormented with desire, Lizzie wanted more. Lizzie required Rose to prove to her by demonstration just how indebted she was, so Lizzie stepped closer. Lizzie pulled Rose's chin up to her wetness. Rose let out a glorious sound as her tongue unfolded to taste. Lizzie's face was glowing as Rose extended her tongue to trace. The spectators kept chanting, the music grew louder. Petting Rose's hair, Lizzie moved in a bit closer, opening her legs wider as she took the seat behind her. Lizzie draped her legs on either chair arm as she did before, demanding Rose's full attention.

The chosen one's rhythm increased, as Rose let out a wondrous howl. Rose gasped for breath. Lizzie, enjoying the heat, required Rose's full attention. Rose's tongue teased Lizzie, as Lizzie grabbed a handful of Rose's hair. Her tongue soon captured her wetness perfectly as Lizzie watched her rhythm. Lizzie shifted slightly to guide Rose's tongue, which was swabbing in all the right places. Rose's ravenous enthusiasm wildly excited Lizzie. Her juices began to flow as

Rose's tongue flatly massaged her. Rose circled the inside of her wetness, as her tongue toggled and flickered madly. Lizzie's moans crescendoed as she slumped forward, reaching her explosive splendor. Rose sucked gently as she rapidly realized that she was echoing Lizzie's moment. Desperately looking up to find Lizzie's approval, their eyes locked, and Rose and her chosen one orgasmed in harmonious exhaustion. The music began to fade, and the spectators became calm.

# CHAPTER 8
## Jim's Stage

Lizzie gathered her dress and champagne, her two guards appearing without being summoned. She slipped back into her dress and began walking. But her mask was much larger and more extravagant than before. It was adorned with far more feathers than she had previously noticed. She had on long, black silk gloves now, which were not previously a part of her wardrobe. And she also noticed her lipstick was a much brighter shade of red, more like a fire-engine red, a shade she never even knew she had.

Lizzie left the velvet room and gravitated toward the music in the next room. Two beautifully voluptuous women, masked, stood in the entrance. One was very tall and thin, like a model, with blonde wavy hair which draped down to her waist. The other was just as tall, dark straight hair in a high ponytail, and she was stroking the other's arm with her extremely long nails. They wore only red garters with red fishnet stockings and red choker necklaces. They walked immediately up to Lizzie's guards, draped their arms around them and fondled them. With the escorts distracted, Lizzie could go farther into the room alone.

A thin layer of smoke covered the floor. Several large, wrought iron cages were placed throughout the room. In each cage, different explicit sexual activities were taking place, numerous others watching, kissing each other, fondling, whatever the moment seemed to call for.

Lizzie noticed a black cat o' nine tails on the table. She picked it up and strutted through the room. The others bowed to her as they passed and she thrilled at her superiority. She would simply acknowledge them with her eyes, yet fail to give them a second glance if their physique didn't entice her. But if there was something about their appearance which appealed to Lizzie, she would graze her flogger down their backside, chest, or breasts, which would bring them to a complete halt, awaiting her command.

Lizzie swaggered by one of the cages; a beautiful black woman kneeling on all fours, with a muscular white man standing in front of her and a very tall, very sleek black man behind her. She was pleasuring the man standing in front of her, as the other man was pounding her from behind. The bars around the cages were wide enough so that the crowd could touch the exhibitionists. Lizzie reached in and flogged the ass of the man railing the beautiful woman. He winced, almost winking at her while he then began to increase his thrusts, throwing the woman into an orgasmic tailspin.

Lizzie made eye contact with the woman, still sucking the hard pole of the man she was pleasing, in obvious hopes it would elevate Lizzie's interest. And it did. Their eyes were glued to each other. Lizzie glared at her, stepping immediately up to the cage, gripping the bars above her head, legs splayed. Another unknown person breathed on her neck, goosebumps rising up over her body. The heat of the breath lingered down the low back drape of her dress onto her bare skin. Lizzie rounded her back, head falling forward. Lizzie clutched the bars, hands lowering. Somebody's hands lifted her dress from behind, a wet mouth kissed her buttocks. The sharp, wet smack stung her ass cheek, catching her off guard. Lizzie wailed in approval, eyes snapping open. She stood as her dress fell down around her. Lizzie turned around to catch a glimpse of whoever was behind her, but there was nobody there.

A woman spun from the top of another cage, lowered onto a man lying face-up with a very erect penis, as he stroked himself in anticipatory delight. A masked man above the cage watched them in silent satisfaction as he lowered her onto the man beneath. Once perched on his huge penis, the man above let the tightly wound rope go. The swing and the woman spun fast on his long spike, bringing him to a fast and furious orgasm, his body bucking, mouth twisting in a lusty roar.

In the last cage, a beautiful short, red-haired woman was blind-folded, sitting with legs wide open, each foot strapped to the legs of the chair, and her arms tied behind her. Her head was thrown back as four women licked her all over her body. Her breathing became labored, as the gasping moans of her participants echoed.

Lizzie walked past the last cage to a round, black, tufted bed; no rails, no footboard or headboard, just a black velvet tufted bed amid the thin layer of smoke still lingering on the floor. The bed was elevated, soft black lighting illuminating it. A small table sat beside it, and on the table were two full champagne glasses and a gold box. She took the first step up to the velvet tufted bed. The music suddenly stopped. Lizzie looked around, wondering what had happened.

But amid Lizzie's sexploits, my own voice leaked in. *I shouldn't be in here. There's menace here, wickedness, people hiding behind people hiding behind masks hiding behind walls; everything was hidden even amid that secretive display of cunning and carnality. Did I step into an unforeseen or forbidden area?* My heart raced as I heard slight shuffling behind me. I was too afraid to move, thinking, *Where am I? What have I done? Is it too late to flee?*

Every hair on my body stood on end as the looming presence approached from behind. I was terrified, my heart pounding, breath coming quick. All eyes were locked on me.

They were silent, and I didn't know if they were going to close in, or what they'd do after that.

I just stood there, swallowing deeply, wanting but not daring to run. The heat of slow and steady breathing on the back of my ear tingled my skin; *my* skin, not Lizzie's.

*No, no,* I silently screamed, *this is Lizzie's domain, I ... this isn't me, this is Lizzie!* But I could only look around with a sudden feeling of isolation, of helplessness. *What do these people want from me? Why do they know who I am?*

*Where's Jim?*

They seemed to be getting closer, a thick wall of robes and masks, dead eyes staring, mumbling and muttering rising around me.

*Lizzie,* I silently shouted out, *don't abandon me now! I need your help!*

"*Shhhhhhhhh ...* "

I caught a hint of a familiar cologne, and instantaneous relief surged through me. Jim guided my glass of champagne to my mouth and I took a drink. He kissed the back of my neck. Taking my glass, he slowly began to trace his fingers up my arms and onto my neck. My lip quivered as my eyes rolled back, marveling in the warmth of his touch.

*Where have you been?* I almost asked. I almost asked myself the same thing. I wanted to turn to face him, but didn't. I couldn't face myself either.

Still braced behind me, Liz and not Lizzie, Jim bowed down to kiss my neck while unzipping the back of my dress. The dress fell to the floor. Jim gently guided my head away from him. Then with one hand, he assertively stroked down my back all the way to my buttocks.

But Lizzie brazenly stood up, feeling her hair plunge back onto his shoulders as she leaned back into him. She threw both her arms over her shoulders to caress Jim's neck, guiding his mouth to her shoulders. Sucking and nibbling on her lip, Lizzie enjoyed the warmth of Jim's fingers circling her firm nipples. His enormous excitement pressed against her buttocks. She melted in his touch. Her every breath hung on his every move. His effect on Lizzie was supernatural. He skillfully controlled her at that moment, as only he could.

And he knew it.

He knew how to play Lizzie, and for the first time in her life, Lizzie didn't mind. Neither Lizzie nor Jim knew for sure who had the upper hand, and as long as they were in the arms of each other, neither cared. No one could please her or quench her desire quite like Jim, and no one piqued his interest or stroked his ego quite like Lizzie. The way they spoke without saying a word, the way they danced without moving, to watch them together, was nothing short of magical. Their chemistry entranced the room.

The music played softly in the background, as Lizzie could hear the shuffling of the others as they moved closer to the big black bed. She only cared about Jim's heavy breathing against her skin. My skin begged for every touch. My body groaned for every movement.

But Lizzie was the one stepping forward to receive it.

He kissed and then gently bit her shoulder as she stroked the back of his neck. She tried to face him, but he wouldn't let her. Forcefully pleasing her wetness, Lizzie began to softly yearn, rhythmically moving with his every contact. She desperately wanted to look into his eyes, anxious to taste his lips, but he wouldn't allow it. He pulled her up a bit so she could feel his anxious manhood. His hand over her mouth kept her from vocal expression of any sort. This only further intensified her desire.

Jim turned Lizzie around, lifted her up, and carried her up the step to the bed. The crowd chanted their approval. The music became louder and pulsated throughout the room. She opened her eyes to see his smoldering look was stern and unyielding. His new mask was large with golden detail, only covering his eyes. His sculpted naked body was oiled with a slight shimmer, as he towered over Lizzie. Even she wasn't sure what to do. She sat on the edge of the bed, raw, naked, and awaiting his commands. The crowd fondled and pleased each other in wild celebratory delight.

A stunning, long-haired blonde woman walked up behind Jim. She peered at Lizzie as she quietly walked around to the opposite side. She wore a large multi-colored feathered mask and a choker necklace. Lizzie sat on the edge of the bed, facing Jim as he grabbed his stiffness. I smiled at him as I opened my mouth.

Lizzie circled the tip with my tongue when he sighed. She took him in farther, circling my tongue around him, gripping him with my lips. Jim's eyes watched her take him deeper inside her hot mouth as his hand cupped the backside of her head, pushing her head forward. Lizzie found him firm and low within her throat, as she felt the soft caress of a hand on my shoulder. Lizzie kept my moist rhythm as Jim moaned. He pushed her back as the woman pulled back my arms and strapped my arms above my head. A large mirror hung on the ceiling above us. Jim pushed her knees up as he intently stroked the inside of Lizzie's thighs. He must have known how much watching was going to turn her on. This man wanted her to watch everything. Just knowing that he wanted Lizzie and Liz to watch was almost as thrilling to Lizzie as actually seeing it myself. We were both thrilled with the taboo of watching.

Jim traced Lizzie's outer wetness, his middle finger slowly slid inside her, his thumb circling the moistness. He licked and kissed her inner thighs as his fingers worked their magic.

Lizzie closed her eyes to absorb the stirring inside her, as she tasted the sugary taste of lips brushing. Lizzie looked up into the mirror to see the blonde leaning over me. She saw the outline of her back as her hair draped across my breasts with a gentle, featherlike sensation.

Jim's head lowered as his lips wandered her thighs, slowly making their way down. Lizzie's muscles tensed as he tormented me with desire. His tongue tapped me as she moaned. The other woman outlined my lips with her tongue. Giggling in delight she pulled Lizzie's face over to hers as she forced her tongue inside our mouth.

Liz couldn't have been less interested. My entire focus was on Jim. This deeply frustrated her but excited him all the more. And Lizzie just loved it!

The line between Liz and Lizzie became increasingly blurred as a certain strength began to well up in my body, fueling Liz and Lizzie both, each rising to the mantle of their sultry inspiration.

Our entire body ached for him. Jim retrieved my glass and poured champagne into our open mouth. He smiled a devilish grin as he offered more, and then more. Quenching our immediate thirst, he dribbled champagne over our breasts, down our stomach, and let it roll down our hot slit. Our new partner was elated with excitement as she saw our excitement show through the hardness of our nipples. She began sucking up the champagne which had been drizzled over them. We couldn't help but groan. Her enthusiastic tongue flicked and tapped our body, one woman licking two without even knowing it, an unwitting orgy all its own. Her fingers pinched and twisted our nipples in a peculiarly painful pleasure. She removed our hand straps. However, Lizzie quite enjoyed them. So Lizzie found her arms back above her head as the blonde firmly held her hands.

Jim placed the champagne glass on the table and opened the gold box. He pulled out a string of beads from the box. Lizzie couldn't contain her excitement, licking her lips and taking over once again. Submissive Liz could only sit back and watch in amazement.

The gaze between Lizzie and the blonde woman never broke. Lizzie found herself on her back and her arms made their way above her head, as the blonde firmly held her hands again. Lizzie swayed back and forth in fiery anticipation, while the crowd began to slowly close in.

Numerous hands moved slowly down her face to her neck, as she arched her back. Hands traced the curves of her large, firm breasts as Lizzie cried out. The blonde covered her mouth with hers in an effort to silence Lizzie. The two began sucking on each other's lips, as Jim knelt down to passionately lick Lizzie's juices. She felt hands on her feet, then her legs as they slowly massaged upward. The music got louder as Lizzie was thrown into a pulsating thrust of movements she couldn't fully understand. The hot moisture of tongues stroked her body. Jim's sweet tongue thrilled her as he slid his finger inside her again. Lizzie smelled the sweetness of the crowd's sexual pleasure as the moans of the others intensified. Jim's heat inside her was so powerful that Lizzie couldn't refrain. Her back arched abruptly and she squirmed as the blonde began wickedly giggling from assisting in Lizzie's gyrating agony.

Jim's tongue massaged Lizzie, then parted her cheeks. He introduced the beads one at a time, deep inside her exit, leaving a slight hang for his convenience later. It was the strangest sensation Lizzie had ever felt. Yet, anything Jim wanted to explore was completely acceptable to her. The blonde let go of Lizzie's arms and slowly stepped back with her head down, as Jim moved in.

I tried to insinuate myself, to push Lizzie aside, but she was too strong willed, determined. *Is this the central struggle of my life,* I had to ask myself, *even then bound and blindfolded. Is this more than just a hint of what my life has become? Is it Alzheimer's or schizophrenia that has me in its grip? If I can overpower this Lizzie, finally take my life back from her once and for all, maybe I'll be cured, maybe I'll be able to have my life back!*

His tongue swiped her lips and met them eagerly with hers. His affectionate, masculine fingers gradually making their way up her legs to her thighs as they opened for him. She was still passionately kissing Jim, as she felt so many hands on her body it was hard to keep track. There were so many different sensations of caressing, licking, and massaging from the crowd. Lizzie knew she wasn't the only one enduring the ecstasy of passion, which turned her on even more. Her hands made their way from her breasts to her sides, where she found her fingers moving through a head of long hair, as they moved her fingers into their mouths. Meanwhile, there was another set of hands on her breast, tongues on her other breast, and soon the hot wet tingle of breath nearing her steaming wetness below. Jim kept kissing her, much more deeply. The delight of the participant below was loud, as she could hear his moans. Female moans leaked in from below. Lizzie couldn't tell which participant was doing what, and she didn't care.

She certainly wasn't going to give up the field to me! I was stuck, lost in the crowd, practically tied up and bound myself, unable to do more than watch this woman run away with my man, my life, my mind! I strained to overcome the shackles that held me, to bite through the gag that pinned my tongue. But the bounds which held me were greater than those which restrained Lizzie. She was loving it, and she

THE VELVET ELITE: Unforgettable Love / Waterford

knew she could break away at any time.

But I was being slowly strangled, driven into the wastelands of my own stolen mind.

Jim broke the seal of their kiss as she saw him stand up to watch the hot tongues devouring her juices. One tongue began to lap up every bit of her juicy wetness, craving more for themselves. A different tongue found the bottom of her thigh while pushing her legs straight up in the air. The tongue began to suck on her buttocks, as another set of hands closed her legs, as if to only tease her further. Lizzie moaned again, Jim whispering, *"Shhhhhhh,"* behind her ear. She did as he asked, then she felt Jim's tongue force open her mouth again. He eased her head back. The rush of the tongue vibrations below, the enforced silence, only further turned her on. Somebody pulled Lizzie's legs back down to the bed, keeping them bent at the knee. Several tongues danced all around her hips, flickering all around her succulent secret, in and out, gently around and around. Her hands were now freely moving on either side as her fingers were entering mouths, as though it were the gentlest way of binding her without force. It was as if they could read her mind; as soon as she would near the brink of no return and finally release the flow of ecstasy, the flickering of tongues would stop and the next participant would eagerly take their place.

Each player had been given the opportunity to please Lizzie, as if she'd been an offering to the crowd. Jim bent down to kiss her, and anyone else involved in playing their game failed to matter. Jim was in command, and the only thing that mattered was he was under Lizzie's spell. He moved to position himself near her head and moved in so she could feel his hardness. Her mouth was open and he slid his throbbing self into her mouth. With her head tilted back and Jim standing behind her head, she eagerly began to lick him while his hand guided her. This was a different sensation, as he entered Lizzie's mouth upside down. He drizzled more champagne around Lizzie's lips, as she attempted to lap it up.

Lizzie's mouth wet and her tongue throbbing, she massaged Jim's penis as he pulled in and out of her mouth, deeper down her throat. He could see how deeply she was taking him, as her throat expanded with each thrust. He would teasingly offer more nectar, dripping slightly on her lips, as he groaned passionately while Lizzie thrust her head back more and more to take him deeper. Lizzie knew he would soon approach the point of no return so she teasingly pulled away. Jim leaned down to her as she whispered, *"Shhhhh,"* in his ear. Jim smiled to realize that she was every bit as into this as he was. They were in this for each other. Everyone else was merely a pawn in their game. And they seemed to love it. They wanted to play, to watch and be watched, and they made the rules.

But instead of relief, I was flooded with heat and the thrush of strength, of a clearing fog. *No,* I shouted to Lizzie, *you back off! This is my moment! I'm the one with Jim, not Beth Ann and not Lizzie either. For good or ill, this is my life, and I'm going to live it! This is my man now, and nobody else is going to have him ... not even me!*

But I was helpless. I tried to reach out and push Lizzie away, force her into the shadows, not the darkness. I tried to scream out to send her fleeing for her life. But it was as if I was in one of those dreams when the limbs are cloaked with lead, too heavy to move, no breath to push the cries out of a tired, dying throat. The harder I tried, the greater the morass around me and beneath me, until all I could do was watch my man cheat on me with myself, in full view of everybody we knew. It was surreal, but it was as real as it could be.

*Or is it? Is this the drugs creating these wild*

*hallucinations? Are we in the throes of some LSD trip, spiked through the robes or masks? That must be it!*

But it was too late to do anything about it, no matter how hard I tried. Soon enough, it became a labor just to keep breathing behind that mask, heart beating faster.

Lizzie felt a release of the massages and tongues all around her. Jim's kisses slowly lingered down her neck to her chest, as she felt his tongue circling her nipples. He worshipped her, and she him. She began to moan loudly, and he didn't seem to mind. His hands traced her breasts as he began to walk beside her toward her feet, never taking his eyes off her. The crowd stepped back into their own crowd of sensual pleasure.

But if I couldn't conquer Lizzie, Jim certainly could. What was more, he seemed to enjoy doing it. He delighted in Lizzie's dark side. It challenged him, it brought out facets of his personality which he normally kept restrained. But he couldn't be a nice guy all the time.

And Lizzie was glad of it. She was thrilled!

"Get on your knees." All eyes turned to them. The echo of Jim's voice shocked and thrilled Lizzie. She changed her position to be on all fours. His hot wet tongue circled her buttocks as he pulled her closer to him. Lizzie felt the sting of Jim's hand smack hard against her buttocks. Lizzie gasped sharply, as Jim soothingly rubbed the affected area. Jim thrust open her thighs with his right hand, as his left adored her long blonde hair cascading down her back. He tugged her hair, as her hot wetness welcomed his rock hard unit. This was all she had truly been waiting for.

Jim teased her implicitly. He thrust in and out. As he pulled out he smacked Lizzie's ass a little bit harder. Lizzie quietly cried out, he gave it a little rub. Then he smacked her again, even harder. Lizzie moaned, "Give me more … " It was just the two of them contributing in play at the moment, but they could hear the crowd chanting around them. This seemed to turn Jim on. Lizzie could feel him getting harder and harder. With both hands on her hips, he pulled her toward him as he thrust deeper, harder, until they nearly reached their climactic moment. Jim pulled the string slowly. This sent shockwaves throughout both of their bodies. Lizzie sensed Jim could feel the internal sensation of the beads every bit as much as she could, and they both let out the most euphoric moan in complete synchronicity. This was unlike any orgasm she had ever experienced before. Exhausted in her weakness, Lizzie collapsed on the bed.

# CHAPTER 9
## The Book

"Hey, you," Jim sweetly whispered. Setting a cup of coffee by the bed, he asked, "How did you sleep?" My painful groan must have been the answer he expected, because he said only, "I thought so. I have aspirin here too if you need it." I opened one eye briefly, then attempted to roll back over.

"Where the hell am I?"

"You're in the guest room. It's okay."

"Oh my God, my aching head," I whined.

Jim chuckled. "I get it. Mine too. But it was a great evening, wonderful event."

"Event?" But he only smiled, offering no other answer. There was little else to say or do but look around the room. "This bed is amazing."

"Feel like having a late lunch and going for a ride in a while?" he asked.

"Uhhh, late lunch?"

"It's half past noon!"

I washed down the aspirin with coffee and lay in bed for a while. My head was pounding and my body was sore. And my mind was an absolute scramble. *Did we really do those things last night? Did that even happen, or did I just imagine the whole thing? Is this coffee drugged too? What the hell is going on here?*

I thought about it, setting the coffee down. *I have to see a doctor,* I realized. *First of all, no telling what I may have picked up at that weird orgy; not from Jim, of course. But who*

*knows what was on a towel or a doorknob or who knows?
Better safe than sorry.*

But I also knew there were more pressing reasons than
that.

*Lizzie,* I thought as I climbed out of bed and made my way
to the changing area outside the bathroom. Reassuring
myself, I vowed, *that's never going to happen again! At first
it was just a thing to do, I guess, a device of some kind, a way
to let myself get a little crazy and not have to take too much
responsibility. Hey, I had imaginary friends when I was a kid,
so what? My teachers all said it was a mark of intelligence.*

But it was Lizzie's voice that answered. *Yeah, sure it is.
You keep thinking that ... until the next time.*

I looked into the mirror again, but the sassy, bitchy
expression that greeted me wasn't my own. She looked like
me, she even sounded a bit like me. But that wasn't me in that
mirror, and it was so clear and so real that it couldn't have
been a dream or a vision or anything but an undeniable truth.

Lizzie smiled at me from the other side of the glass. *First
of all, Liz, you better knock it off with that doctor shit. They'll
put us somewhere dark and lonely. Maybe they'll let Prince
Charming visit on Saturdays, the two of you can sit and color
together. That might be fine for little Miss Mousy, but I need
more than that. I'm not gonna rot in some asylum, I can
promise you that! You let them drag you away, I'll stay out
here and have him all to myself!*

I looked at that woman in the mirror, barely recognizing
her face as my own. Shuddering to anticipate the answer, I
put the question to her which had to be asked. *Did I ... did
you kill Beth Ann?* Lizzie just laughed, throwing her head
back a bit, wickedness in her witch's cackle. *You did, didn't
you? You threw her off that cliff so you could have Jim. Admit
it, you murdered her!*

But Lizzie just kept laughing, that mirror an impenetrable barrier between them.

Anger rose up in me like I'd never known, frustration and rage and hatred against that bitch of a woman who was ruining my life. I grabbed the hair dryer, the nearest thing to me of any size or heft, and smashed it into Lizzie's face. The mirror shattered, lines instantly reaching out like a deranged spider's web, fragmenting my reflection into a chaotic, mosaic, monstrous version of myself.

But Lizzie was gone, at least for the time being. There was little I could do but hope she'd stay away and resolve to beat her back the next time she dared to rear her ugly, beautiful head.

I found some more clothes in the chest of drawers and turned on the radio to hear Eric Clapton's "It's in the Way That You Use It".

Still shaken from what had happened in the bathroom, I looked for Jim in the living room, but he wasn't there. I had no idea how I'd explain the broken mirror to him. *He's so kind and caring,* I reassured myself, *he won't mind. He is smart, I had to agree with myself, but that means he'll know, it means he knows what's going on, with Lizzie and the cabal, the memory loss. He'll see that mirror and know things are just getting worse.*

I looked outside the kitchen window and saw no sign of him. But I was still upset and needed something just to quiet my nerves. I needed to eat something, drink something, *do* something to feel like I was moving forward with a life that at least resembled normalcy. And I was really getting hungry, so I raided the refrigerator. I pulled out some sliced turkey and vegetables and looked around for bread. A note on the fridge read, *Got a call. Ran into town. Be back soon.* So I shrugged and made my sandwich. I stood at the kitchen island and ate half of it. I took the second half and took a closer look at his big book collection.

Next to the bookcase a photo hung on the wall, a man and a woman Liz didn't quite recognize. They stood together, smiling at whomever happened to be on the other side of that glass.

She was pretty, earthy, a long chestnut mane cascading over her shoulders. *Wait, do I know her? We're friends, from ... from college?*

The man was ruggedly handsome, dark hair, dark eyes, and a complexion most men would give their eye teeth to have.

My mind flashed with strange visions; a dark room, two costumed figures on each side of me, hands gliding over my flanks and thighs and breasts. Their faces were covered by plastic masks, featureless, but the hair seemed familiar.

*Under the hoods? Were they wearing robes?*

But it just didn't make sense. I chalked it up to my imagination, which was obviously working overtime for some reason. *Could it be the change of season or daylight savings time? That always throws me a bit.* Reassured, I moved on to the bookcase.

He had first editions of an old nineteenth century copy of Mark Twain's *The Adventures of Tom Sawyer* and many other classics. He had an antique quill with a crystal inkwell setting on one of the shelves, an old book press.

The spine of one particular book wasn't anything particularly beautiful, and it didn't exactly stand out in any impressive sort of way. But the title caught my eye: *Book* in bold, old-world, red lettering. I brushed my hands free of any crumbs and pulled the book down. It was just a little stuck, so I tugged it a bit. But instead of pulling the book out, a secret doorway opened up behind the bookcase to my left. I jumped back, frightened that I had broken something or done something wrong. My jaw dropped sharply, and my eyes widened in shock. The book immediately pulled itself back and resumed its original position.

Nearly terrified of what I'd done, and not having any idea of how in the world I was going to fix this, my curiosity pushed me closer to the hidden doorway. Lizzie abruptly woke up. *You idiot. Now look what you've done! How are you gonna explain this?* My heart was absolutely pounding. I knew this gargantuan house was very old, but I never would have anticipated anything like a secret door. I stepped slowly and quietly. I walked to the opening to peek in, but it was too dark inside to see very much.

*Well,* Lizzie chided me, *go in!* So I pushed the book-lined doorway open a bit more, peering in carefully to see.

I felt that I was on the verge of a discovery, one which had been evading me with maddening persistence. The secret to what I was doing in that house was somewhere in that basement. But I had to wonder, *why is it such a secret? Why isn't Jim being more forthcoming? He knows the answer, he must! I was a guest at his wedding, so he must know ... the origin of our friendship, how long it's been since his wife died.*

*How did she die?* I had to wonder again, and with greater energy. *Surely he didn't have anything to do with it. Or ... did he? I wouldn't have thought it, dreamt it, even dared to imagine it of such an obviously decent and warmhearted man.*

*But ... is he that, or is that just a front? Would a sweet, kind man take a woman to such a depraved experience as we had last night? That's not exactly* The Brady Bunch *or* Father Knows Best. *Maybe this nice-guy routine is just a cover for his dark side, perhaps very dark. Is that what happened to Beth Ann? There must be some connection somewhere, I know*

75

*it, I can feel it in my bones! Did she find out about his weird double-life? Did he have to silence her somehow? If so, what's he planning to do with me?*

*No,* I told myself, *not Jim. He's just not that type of person! He's a good man, I know he is.*

But it was Lizzie's voice that answered, skepticism ripe in her world-weary voice. *Sure, a good man with a secret basement, a mysteriously vanished ex-wife, and a cabal of sexual deviants ... that's a real good man you found there, Liz. I only hope you can handle yourself.*

More flashes of remembered moments filled my mind's eye, those two costumed figures bending me over a big table, hands on my hips, my legs splayed.

A car door slammed outside. I froze. *Oh shit!* Lizzie yelled, *OMG, hurry! Shut the door!*

My heart was beating out of my chest as I looked around, trying to figure out what to do. I tried to close the door, but there was no knob or handle or anything. So I pulled on the bookshelf. It was very heavy, but I pulled until I heard it latch. *Thank God!* I ran to the kitchen island where all my sandwich ingredients were still sitting just as Jim walked in.

"Well hey there, beautiful!" He walked in carrying a bag of groceries. I smiled to greet him. He took off his baseball cap and sat the groceries next to me. He paused for a second. "You okay? Something wrong?" he asked, as a look of worry swept across his face.

Nervously, I looked at him. "No, I'm fine. Why do you ask?"

He pulled some fresh berries from the bag and looked at me. "I don't know. You just look a little pale. Sure you're feeling okay?"

"Oh yes, I'm fine." I started to clean up the mess I had made while he put away the groceries. I kept looking over to the bookcase, all the while trying to not make it seem obvious. I was just hoping and praying it wasn't blatantly obvious that I had accidentally stumbled upon something I shouldn't have. I couldn't help obsessing over what lay behind that bookcase.

# CHAPTER 10
## Amazement

"Okay, wanna go for a ride?" Jim asked.

I turned and smiled. "I'd love to." I grabbed my purse sitting on the kitchen island, and we hopped in the Speedster.

We took a right at the fork and drove north. The sun shined brightly over the hills, golden and gorgeous. We took some winding backroads and passed grapevine-lined roadsides. The red, orange, and yellow leaves whirled by. I wasn't sure if it was the beautiful scenery, the sunny day, or just merely being together, but the contentment in our smiles best described what a beautiful day it truly was.

The crisp, autumn air was invigorating. Vineyards spread out around us on either side, strewn with grapevines in precise rows, caking rolling foothills under the clear blue sky.

We drove over the top of one mountain to see the beautiful Pacific Ocean stretched out in front of us and a small seaside town on the shore. I knew this was where Jim was taking me, but I still had no idea why.

We took a left down a twisting road. But this was no tourist trap, just a little artsy town. The locals smiled and waved as we drove past. Sunflower stands and pumpkin markets brought me back to a different world, a simpler time. Children hopped around their parents, their little faces painted like cats, bunnies, or other cute animals by the local face-painter. We passed a beautiful market.

Music got louder the farther into town we drove, until we pulled up to a parking lot with a banner over the entrance reading, *Grand Fall Art & Music Festival.*

Jim asked, "Up to it?"

My eager nod was the only answer he needed. We parked, and he took me by the hand to lead me into the clamor of the crowd. The performer's stage was about fifty yards to our right, the crowd mingling in the central area, and a row of booths and other attractions to our right.

A very charming pumpkin patch was cluttered with Cinderella pumpkins, shorter and wider and brighter than the taller, more circular pumpkins used for jack-o-lanterns. People went around picking them by hand, right off the vine.

We snacked on cotton candy and caramel apples, arm-in-arm, giggling like love-struck teenagers. There was no mistaking the magnetism between us. We were fully enjoying being together, we were captivated by one another.

A painted wooden sign read, *Biggest Corn Maze In History! 30 Acres of Maze-citement.* I'd always wanted to experience a corn maze. "Oh, Jim, we *have* to go in," I yelped, practically giddy with exhilaration as I tugged on his arm.

"Sure, of course," he acknowledged, with the widest schoolboy grin I'd ever seen.

I took off running ahead of him. My heart was pounding, I was dizzy with excitement. I turned a corner, assuming he was right on my heels, and then turned another.

"Jim, isn't this amazing?" But no answer came back. I turned with a sudden start to see that he wasn't there. I was alone and lost. "Jim?"

The music in the background was pretty loud, so he obviously didn't hear me. The corn walls of the maze were so tall and dense that I couldn't see through them. My heart started to pound. *Thirty acres? I could die in here!*

I turned around to go back, but I couldn't recall exactly if I'd made a left and then a right, or a right and then a left.

*Relax,* Lizzie told me in the back of my brain, *you're a grown woman, for Chrissake! The entrance isn't far back there. Somebody'll come along and give directions back. Jim will be there waiting!*

But nobody came. The only sound was of the music beyond the maze.

"Jim? Jim!" I could hear the worry rising in my voice.

I stumbled around a few corners heading back, at least I thought I was heading back. But I wound up drilling myself deeper into the maze until I found a bench which I didn't recognize. *At least I can rest a bit, wait here, Jim will come along ... or somebody will.*

But as the moments passed, my hands started to sweat, my heart beat faster, panic shooting through my brain, nerves crackling under the skin. I closed my eyes and thought, *When I open them, Jim will be here.*

I felt a shadow over me. I felt Jim's lips brush against mine. I pulled my hand up over my eyes in an effort to shade the sun's glare when I saw Jim towering over me. He leaned back down, kneeling next to me, pulling me on top of him, as we lay next to the bench on the ground.

My hair fell around his face, as he pushed it back with his hand to kiss me. Jim's tongue traced my lips, as he kissed me. His breathing deepened as he slid his tongue inside my shaking lips, tugging on my hair a bit. I opened my eyes to catch a glimpse of this incredibly handsome man, as his eyes penetrated acutely into mine. He groaned softly, as he pulled me around and under him. Jim pressed hard against me. He was ready. We didn't know if anyone would walk up to see us, and neither one cared. Still kissing, he unbuttoned my blouse and freed the front snap of my bra. My breasts firmly broke loose. His mouth dropped down to cradle my firm nipple, which was begging to feel his tongue. He scooped me up, plopped himself down on the bench, straddling my legs around him. He was watching my expression, never breaking his stare, as he removed his leather jacket and unbuttoned his shirt. My whole body trembled with excitement.

He leaned down to kiss me, as I could feel the texture of his unbuttoned shirt on my breasts. He unbuttoned with one hand and unzipped my jeans with the other while I sat straddling him. Sucking on my lip, he inserted his middle finger into my mouth, as I began to massage his manhood. He then took that finger and slid it into my panties, thrusting it inside my wetness. My head plunged back as he passionately kissed my neck, while his finger massaged inside. A full body wave of heat sent shockwaves through every cell of my body as my muscles began to tense.

He quietly whispered in my ear, "I want you." I pulled his face to mine, looked soulfully into his eyes, inaudibly returning his desire. His deep melodic massage lit a fire inside me. He was fully capable of instinctively reading my body's innermost rhythms.

He flung his jacket on the ground, pulled me up, and gently lay me down on top of it. On his knees, he began to pull my jeans down past my knees. I bit my lower lip. Panting and gasping for air, I looked at him.

He peered down to me. "I want to hear you beg," A moment of silence passed and he went on, "I'll give you what you want. Just let me hear you beg."

"Please?" But I knew it wasn't enough. "Please," I repeated, then louder, "Please!"

He smiled just a bit. "Turn over."

I rolled over on all fours. He pulled my G-string over to one side as he smacked my ass. "Beg me."

"Please?" I asked yet again.

"You can do better than that!"

"*Ooooh pleeeeeeezzzzzzzz?*"

"Oh yes, that's my girl." He tugged my hair and rubbed my ass. I was nearing my elation before he even slid inside me. He smacked my ass again, then rubbed it soothingly. The sting and sooth sent me over the edge as he thrust his rock hard unit inside me. He tugged my hair, and I let out a deep groan, my muscles squeezing his throbbing vein inside me. Jim pulled my hips forcefully against his as he slid in and out rhythmically, deeper and harder.

But he stopped suddenly.

"No," I rasped, "don't stop … please … don't … stop … "

He pulled my legs apart a bit more, as he leaned down and around to massage my wetness as he entered me again. His fingers massaged all the right places as he plunged inside me. I was so wet, his hardness gliding in and out, I moaned, louder than I expected.

Controlling the rhythm, Jim arched his back as we both felt the hot wet impact of unthinkable orgasm between us. It poured and gushed between us, his juices flowing with my own, splashing against the walls of my body, my soul. He was pouring out into me and I was being completely filled by his essence, his power, his energy and strength.

Our breathing slowed, yet neither of us moved from that position. Endorphins rushed through our bodies. I let out a huge sigh as I lowered my head down to rest on my hands. Lizzie seemed completely satisfied with my performance.

We finally made our way out of the gigantic corn maze, hand-in-hand, smiling and catching each other's glances along the way. We held hands while spending the rest of the afternoon and early evening walking through the festival, even during our ride on *The Scrambler.*

We smiled and laughed almost to the point of tears. We walked around, shared popcorn, enjoyed a hay ride. With only a few of us seated on a massive trailer covered in hay bales, we all had plenty of room to spread out. Jim sat on a bale of hay, and I lay my head in his lap chewing on a straw of hay, staring up at the beautiful sky. Jim looked down at me with those wonderful blue eyes, brushed his thumb on my chin and whispered, "I love you, Liz."

I must have had a look of shock on my face, as my mouth fell open. My heart leaped into my throat. I thought, *Oh my god, did he really say what I thought I heard him say?* I sat up. Without caring who was around us or what they may think, I moved over and straddled Jim while he sat on the bale of hay. He chuckled for a moment, then placed his hands on my hips.

I cradled this beautiful man's face in my hands and responded, "I love you, too, Jim." He smiled at me as we shared a tender kiss. The other hayride passengers smiled at us and we blushed.

The hayride mercifully ended and Jim jumped off first, then held his hand out to help me down.

We walked back toward the car. I leaned over and playfully smacked his butt. With a little growl, he scooped me up as I let out a squeal. Jim slid me down on the passenger's side convertible door through the opened window. He gazed into my eyes as he ran his fingers through my hair. He pulled me tightly to his lips, like heaven on earth to me. We made out like high schoolers, not having a care in the world. The moment couldn't have been anymore poetic as our kiss ended while the sun began to set.

The autumn air sent a chill down our spines, so Jim put the top up on the car and we rolled up the windows. We didn't share another word the entire way home. With all the smiles and glances and hand-holding, there was no need to talk.

Back at the house, we walked in the back door to the

kitchen. I looked over, and the very first thing to capture my attention was that irritating bookcase. I couldn't help but stare at it, and I found myself even more curious as to what possibly could be behind it.

Jim looked at me, holding his hand out to me. "Stay right there. I'll be back in just a minute."

# CHAPTER 11
## The Awakening

I walked to the bookcase, curious if I had time to pull the book back out and look a little more deeply inside the doorway. However, I was too worried it would either be too noisy or I wouldn't have enough time, so I didn't. I just looked around again. I found myself walking up to the painting again of the little blonde ballerina. She was so lovely. But she seemed so sad. I stood there … staring, just like the ballerina herself, gazing at something unknown, something otherworldly.

Jim walked up behind me. "Whatcha thinking about?"

"Oh, um, I dunno," I began. "She is just so beautiful. I can't help but wonder why she looks so sad."

"Well, I do know she missed her mother terribly," he began. He shoved both hands into his front pockets as he cleared his throat. "She and her mom planted a peony garden just outside her bedroom window." He smiled. "There were always colorful butterflies hovering around the garden." His voice cracked a bit as he continued. "Her profile at this moment was just so entrancing. I wanted to capture that moment."

I said, "I'll bet she looks just like her mother."

He turned to me, touched my cheek and said, "Yes, oh yes. She most certainly does." I leaned into the warmth of his chest.

I had to ask. "What happened … to her, I mean, your wife?"

Jim paused for a moment, then cautiously answered, "Amanda, err Mandy, and her mother were so close." His eyes looked back at the painting. "They were more than close, almost twin souls."

I put my hand through his arm, while his hands remained in his front pocket.

"My wife suffered from early onset Alzheimer's and dementia. Mandy had the hardest time of it, feeling so helpless. Watching her mother deteriorate right in front of her eyes. It was … it was heartbreaking for her, more than anyone. Being so close and seeing emptiness in her mother's eyes … it was just way too much." Tears welled up in his eyes. "So she … she had to get away from it, to close herself off from it, the hurt, the disease, the pain, all of it." His lip quivered, his expression became solemn. "You want so badly to figure out a way … anything. But it's a life of fruitless desperation, I'm afraid." He turned to me. "I loved my wife so much. I tried to figure out a way to consistently be an active part in the world she was forced to live in."

I touched his face.

"I probably could have dealt with another man in her life," he went on, "but to be defeated by something I couldn't see or fully understand? It was the most difficult thing to cope with, something so foreign and completely devastating. I only wanted to keep a part of her with me, in my life, in *our* lives, that I would have literally done anything at all to help her," he affirmed emotionally. Tears ran down his cheeks, vulnerability in his throat as he tried to fight it. I was paralyzed, I felt as helpless to help him as he must have felt to help his wife. There was nothing I could say. The best I could do was to listen, and to care.

"Beth Ann wasn't responsible for what happened to her. She didn't ask for that. She didn't understand or even realize how quickly she was deteriorating. It came like a thief in the night. Mandy's mother abandoned her, my wife abandoned me, but Beth Ann had no idea." His eyes now filled with tears, as they steadily flowed down his cheeks as he seemingly became lost in thought. Somehow he managed to quickly regroup, and he leaned his head on my shoulder. "I'm so sorry."

I looked around, not sure how to react. So I just wrapped my arms around him and gave him a big hug. "None of this was your fault, Jim. I'm certain Beth Ann knew how much you loved her. It breaks my heart to see you so sad."

He pulled his forehead off my shoulder and looked at me. "I'm so glad you're here."

I wiped tears from his cheeks, as I kissed his lips softly. "I am too."

We stood lost in the reality of our feelings for each other. I knew I was right where I was supposed to be. I didn't think about where I probably *should* be. The only thing that mattered was where I was and who I was with at that very second.

"I love you, Liz."

"I feel it too." He held my cheeks in his hands as he guided my eyes up to meet his.

"Liz, let's hold onto this moment, always remember where we were at this second in time." This rugged and masculine man was allowing himself to be so vulnerable, yet it was obvious he didn't want to go through another heartbreak. I only knew I would never, *could* never, hurt him. I only wanted to reassure him that I was completely and helplessly in love with him. I responded with, "I will. I'll always remember."

He gave me a tight hug and we walked down the hallway into his bedroom and closed the door.

*

Birds sang right outside Jim's bedroom window, the cool

autumn breeze dancing across my skin. Jim's arm was slung around my waist while we both lay peacefully spooning in his bed.

*Did we make love again last night? I don't remember!*

My mind immediately went to the twisted mysteries of my presence in Jim's house. But things were starting to fall into place, and I felt I was getting closer. Jim lay quietly sleeping, my gaze falling on his calm expression, so at peace.

*He's so unhappy inside*, I had to silently confess. *He obviously loves and misses his wife, who died after a battle with Alzheimer's. She did die, didn't she? Did I know her before I knew Jim? I feel like Beth Ann introduced us, but ... I just can't remember....*

We stirred and Jim leaned in to whisper, "Good morning." I smiled to feel his mouth on my ear. We lay in this massive four-poster bed, practically lost in a bed full of fluffy white pillows and sheets. They were so amazingly soft, it was like I was floating.

He pulled me closer, both of us naked, his morning erection pressing against me. He kissed my neck before climbing out of bed. I just lay there, smiling, looking out the window at the morning sun sneaking through the trees. It was so peaceful and serene. Reflecting on the previous day we spent together, and at how happy I was, a tear of joy rolled down my cheek. I only wanted to stay in this moment forever. I closed my eyes to listen to the birds.

My doubt and wonder seemed to ebb. It was so pleasant to be with Jim. It felt so natural, that it was just easier to let the questions slip away. It was comforting to believe it would all work itself out, that everything would be clear. I was thinking too much, concentrating too hard, worrying about something which surely had some perfectly natural explanation. Looking into Jim's loving gaze, it was easy to accept that, even embrace it.

I felt his hand brush my cheek. "What would you like to do this afternoon?" he asked. I opened my eyes to see that I was on the opposite side of the bed, and the clock read *2:32 p.m.*

A little dazed, I sat up asking, "What the? I swear, I just closed my eyes for a minute."

He smiled, confirming, "I guess you were pretty tired. I let you sleep. You looked so peaceful, I didn't have the heart to wake you." I shot up, wrapped the sheet around me, grabbed the bottle of water on the nightstand, and walked out the bedroom door. "Whatever you wanna do is fine with me."

What I wanted to do and what I needed to do were two entirely different things. I wanted to pull him into bed with me and lie there for days, but what I needed to do was take a shower and clean up. It was obvious he had been up and busy for hours while I slept. I walked down the hallway to my appointed bedroom. I opened my closet door and silently stood there. I had the oddest sensation of *déjà vu*; me, standing in front of my closet.

My bedroom door flew open. Jim poked his head in the door and said, "Hey, I just got a call and I need to run over to the winery for a little bit. You'll be okay while I'm gone?"

I looked over my shoulder at him and smiled. "Sure, of course."

He winked at me, pulled the door closed again while saying, "Okay, I'll see ya later. Won't be too long." My attention went back to the closet, but at that point I had lost the *déjà vu*. I dropped the sheet and walked into the bathroom to turn on the shower. I stood in front of the jagged bathroom mirror, staring at myself. *I wonder if I remind him of his ex-wife. Could I make him as happy as she did?* The steam from the shower fogged the mirror.

The hot water beating down on my neck and shoulders was melodic and relaxing. I must have been in there quite a while because the water soon turned from hot to mildly warm, and then cool.

I stepped out of the shower and slipped into my robe. I bent over, twisted my hair into the towel on top of my head, then walked over to the cracked mirror to wipe the condensation away.

I walked into the kitchen and grabbed a wine glass and glanced at the bookcase. My heart started racing. *Do I have time to check it out again, find out what's back there before Jim gets home? Should I?* The longer I stood, the more anxious I became.

*Give it a try!* Lizzie urged me. *You can't go on not knowing, can you?* In the moments of my consideration, Lizzie groused. *Well, if you won't, I will!*

I tugged on the *Book* and the doorway pressed forward slightly. I took the towel onto a chair and let my damp hair fall. I pushed open the door, a breeze whipping out of the crevice.

In the dark hall behind the bookcase, a chain dangled from a bare bulb affixed to the ceiling.

*Chink!* The bulb lit up.

A wooden staircase led down to my right. The light only reached as far as the bottom of that staircase, where another bulb hung waiting.

I quietly stepped down the stairs, and that bottom chain's bulb lit up the whole room before me. It was a fairly large stone basement full of odds and ends, and it smelled a little musty. Large wooden frames encased old photographs, yellowing behind the glass.

It was cold and damp, concrete floors and ceiling preventing any circulation. My skin crawled, a chill ran up my spine.

One wall had the letters *VE* painted in a fancy, scripted style, white paint on the stone wall. It was almost like an insignia of some sort. A large sturdy wooden table in the center of the room had the same *VE* insignia painted in the middle of the table. I was completely intrigued. *What does it stand for? What's at the bottom of all this?*

There was a set of wooden shelves with framed pictures, but the lighting was too dim and I couldn't make out who was in the photographs. The large candelabras on either side of the table in the center of the room were stunning.

*What's this room used for?*

Dark images, barely lit, returned to my memory, my body being flipped over onto my back, one holding down my wrists, a woman.

I struggle, but I don't mind. I'm being ravaged, and I'm loving it.

I kept looking at that insignia, *V. E.*, which I recognized from the orgy. *It was tattooed on most of the people there ... what does it mean? Is it ... something to do with veterans? What about Beth Ann? Where did she fit into all this? Was she some kind of ... of high priestess, or ... or a human sacrifice?*

More memories flashed across my brain, too fast for me to keep track of them all.

*The other night, at the so-called event, that wasn't my first time there,* I realized. *It wasn't, just like it wasn't my first time at that cliffside! Is there some connection? Was that a site of some bizarre ritual? Is that where Beth Ann met her fate ... and was I somehow involved?*

My heart beat faster. With so many holes in my memory and so much strange new information, my fevered brain couldn't help but jump to the most tantalizing and the most terrifying assumptions.

*And how does all this connect to my weird lapses in memory? Am I being drugged somehow? All that delicious food Jim keeps making, is he really just keeping me doped up, getting me ready for my part in the next big ritual, the next human sacrifice?*

*No, not Jim, not Jim!*

But looking around the dark basement, it was getting harder to resist coming to some logical conclusions. The Jim I knew and had fallen in love with wouldn't have had anything to do with such an arcane cabal, much less a secret room where I'd been taken.

*Or did I lure them there? No, one of them must have been Jim; this is his basement, not mine. Isn't it? Is this the kind of man Jim really is?*

The person I was wouldn't just fall in love with some strange man, and I wouldn't keep forgetting so much about my life. *There's something going on there, and something going on behind it! Whatever is responsible for my memory loss is connected to that cabal somehow.*

I trembled, nausea tightening in my stomach. There was something big happening there and I was close to remembering what it was, and to figuring out why I couldn't remember in the first place.

Jim's words echoed in the back of my head, that his wife had suffered from Alzheimer's and early onset dementia. My blood ran cold as I turned to the imagined visage of Lizzie, my closest confidant and my mortal enemy.

*Is that what's happening to me? Am I ... do I have Alzheimer's? Do I have dementia? That would explain the memory loss for sure.* But it also left a lot unexplained. *Is that how Jim and I met? Did Beth Ann and I undergo some kind of treatment or therapy together, is that how I came to be involved with all this? Did Beth Ann introduce me to Jim?*

*Was she ... was she trying to get me into the cabal?*

Lizzie offered no answer, as if I'd already gained ground against her. I felt that I was already taking my life back, clue by clue, discovery by discovery, and that if Lizzie couldn't hinder me, she certainly wasn't about to help.

*Yes!* I silently exclaimed, *that's it ... no wait, no ... I ... I was already in it?*

I shook my head, confused, unable to wrap my head around the mystery.

My instincts told me I should just turn everything off and go back upstairs. Hairs stood up on the back of my neck. *Jim's nearby.* Lizzie warned me, *Don't let him come down here now, not like this!* I was meddling in things which were absolutely none of my business. So I turned everything off, walked back upstairs, and closed the bookcase.

I grabbed my towel off the chair as Jim walked in the front door, startling me. We always came and went through the kitchen, it only then occurred to me.

He held my shoulders and concernedly asked, "Whoa, you okay?"

"Um, yes," I stammered, "I … I'm fine. Just didn't think you'd be back so soon."

He rubbed my arms. "Didn't really expect to be gone two hours, so I'm sorry about that."

"Two hours?"

He smiled and said, "Yes, I'm so sorry." I attempted to go along with things and not act at all alarmed by the lapse in time, but Jim could read the worry on my face. "You okay?"

"Oh yeah. Yep, I'm fine. I'm going to go dry my hair. I'm freezing."

He walked over to me and touched my hair. "Liz, your hair is dry." I felt my hair, dry beneath my fingers. I pointed to the bookcase and then pointed back over to my room when he asked me, "Honey, you look pale. Are you sure you're okay?"

"Yes, I am. I'm fine. I'm just going to go get dressed now, warm up." He smiled and I could feel his eyes watching me as I walked away and into my room.

I closed the bedroom door behind me. My heart was racing. I stood holding the door knob in one hand and my head resting on my other hand as I tried to retrace my steps.

*I must have been down there for over an hour after my shower,* I knew, *but ... I wasn't, I know that much time didn't pass. It couldn't have! Ten minutes, fifteen tops!*

All I knew is I was extremely cold and needed to get out of that robe and into some clothes. I heard Jim outside the door. "What do you feel like having for dinner?"

*Dinner? I haven't even had breakfast or lunch yet! What do you mean, dinner*? I looked over at the clock on the wall.

6:15.

My blood ran cold. W*hat the hell is going on here? That accident must have really done some damage, there's no point in denying it. I've got to get to a hospital or something, I could be bleeding internally. I could be dying!*

But Lizzie just glared at me from the mirror, shaking her head. *Shake it off, you wimp. You're just afraid of finally getting what you want, what you deserve ... what we both deserve! Why do you ruin every good thing that comes along for us? What's the matter with you, Liz?*

*What's the matter with me,* I wanted to shout back, *I don't really know! That's just the problem, isn't it? If I knew what was really wrong with me, I'd know who I was, I'd know what I'm trying to do here. Where's my real family? Why was I out driving when I passed out, what was I trying to do? There's an answer to all this, I know there is!*

But I was too tired to fight. I finished getting dressed and walked to the kitchen. The scent of sautéed garlic and onions filled the air. Jim had a hand towel slung over his shoulder, humming to music in the background as he cooked. He took a spoonful of sauce from the simmering pot on the stove and blew on it. "C'mere, taste. Tell me what it needs," he said.

I tasted the sauce. "Oh my God, that is so good!"

I sat on one of the island stools, crossed my legs, and took a sip of his wine. I let out a satisfied sigh with the first sip, which prompted Jim to walk around to take a look at me. He smiled, but it soon turned to a slight frown.

I asked, "What's wrong?"

He pointed at my feet. "Guess I need to clean the floors."

I uncrossed my legs to look, and I saw that they were indeed very dirty. *Crap!* I hadn't even thought about checking my feet when I came up from downstairs.

"So," I said, quickly changing the subject, "whatcha go to the winery for? Something going on?"

He shrugged. "Just needed to handle some things, nothing for you to worry about."

I joined him at the stove. "Can I help you with something?"

"Got it covered. You just enjoy the wine and relax." I walked to the island and picked up his wine glass as he poured himself another.

The doorbell rang and Jim went to answer it. "Oh thank you … Yes, yes, perfect. Thanks again," he said. He returned to the kitchen and asked if I was hungry.

"Um, yes, thanks. Who was that? I'm sorry, I don't mean to intrude, you've been so kind...."

"One of the managers from the vineyard," he answered. "I wanted to take you for a drink after dinner, just wanted to make sure the timing was okay with them."

I returned the smile. "That's so sweet. I'd love that."

We ate dinner, and talked, and laughed. There were a few moments when I caught myself laughing out loud at some of the things he was telling me about how he grew up, and some of the things he got away with when he was young. It would make me smile at the mere thought of imagining a much younger version of him, up to youthful shenanigans like throwing rocks at trains, stealing candy from the local shopkeeper.

After dinner, we cleaned the dishes together and headed for the winery.

The beautiful dusk sky was stretched out above us, orange burning into pale purple. Jim led me to the garage and opened the door to reveal a pair of bicycles. I guessed at once that one of the bikes had been his late wife's, but that didn't bother me. I even found it flattering that he would allow me to ride her bike with him.

But a look of worry must have flashed across my face, because he asked, "What's the matter, Liz?"

"Um, I don't know if I can ride a bike anymore, Jim. I mean, I can't tell you the last time I rode one."

He grinned and reassuringly said, "Liz, once you know you never forget. It's like riding a bike … in fact, it *is* riding a bike!" We shared a chuckle. "We can take our time. And it isn't far at all."

I could feel Lizzie punching me inside. *What are you afraid of? Get on!*

I took a quick couple of small laps in his rather large driveway as Jim began riding alongside me. "See, you're doing great!" The autumn breeze blew through my hair, the setting sun's shimmering light bounced around the hills. Jim and I giggled as I nearly lost my balance, but regained it quickly. I breathed in the cool, fresh air as we rode down the dirt road toward the vineyard. We passed a small lake on our right, as Jim looked back to see Layla running playfully to catch up with us. She ran alongside us most of the way to the vineyard, until a gaggle of geese deterred her. Jim just laughed as he let her go on about her business.

We rode around to the beginning edge of the vineyard, when Jim signaled me to follow him through the narrow path between the grapevines. The crisp autumn air carried the smells of the wildflowers and the grapevines. The path ended at the lake we'd passed coming in. A small candle-lit table with two chairs and a bottle of champagne in an ice bucket were waiting for us. A beautiful plaid blanket was laid out next to the table.

Jim rode up ahead, then stopped and turned. "What do you think?"

I struggled to answer. "It's … amazing." I stood in front of him, cradled his face with my hands, and sweetly brushed his lips with mine. He pulled me close, my legs weakening, ears suddenly ringing. It felt as though I were passing out. Jim asked me if I was all right, at least I thought he did. I couldn't hear him. I couldn't feel him. I felt like I'd slipped out of my own body. I couldn't answer, I couldn't speak.

I finally whispered, "I don't feel so well." I looked at him, and everything turned gray and fuzzy.

"Liz." I heard a voice. "Liz, are you okay?" The blurred glare of the moonlight blinded me, and a sweet and muffled little girl's voice asked me gently, *Mommy, are you okay?* The masculine voice overpowered hers when I opened my eyes and attempted to sit up. Feeling a bit nauseous and equally as dizzy, I struggled.

"Easy, baby … easy." Jim looked down at me. The moonlight shined behind him like a halo. I smiled as I raised up in his arms. I looked around for the little girl I heard, but found no trace.

"The little girl," I began.

Jim's brows arched, his mouth in a concerned frown. "What little girl, sweetheart?"

I pointed in the direction of the voice I heard, but there was no one there but Jim. He helped me slowly raise up. I pointed the other direction. "I heard a little girl. She called me *Mommy*."

"Honey, there is nobody else here."

"But I heard her,"

"Maybe you were dreaming?"

"Huh? Were we sleeping?" I looked around a couple more times and finally came to terms with the thought that perhaps he was right. "Okay." But then I heard the echo of her sweet little voice back through the vineyard. I stood up, as Jim nervously tried to keep me lying down.

"No," I murmured. "She's over there. I can hear her." I stumbled toward the grapevines, as I could hear her voice again. *Mommy?*

Jim followed with a feeble, "Liz!" He grabbed my arm.

"No!" I pulled away and kept running. I ran down the pathway between the grapevines toward the dirt road. Jim was close at my heels. I ran to the end of the pathway to the dirt road, when I heard her voice again. I couldn't figure out which direction it was coming from. I turned to the right, then to the left, then turned around to see Jim running toward me. I felt nauseous again, a wave of heat pulsing throughout my body. I turned around and around, sweat dripping down into my eyes. With no sight of the little girl, I turned to see Jim within arm's reach, when I suddenly heard the deafening ringing in my ears again before my body fell hard to the gravel road and everything went black.

I woke to see Jim's blurred silhouette above me. I could see his mouth moving, but it took a few minutes to finally hear his words of complete panic.

"Liz. Liz?" I tried to answer, but somehow the words wouldn't come Finally, I touched his hand as he continued, "Honey, can you hear me?" I looked around me, then back to Jim, as he finally came into focus.

"I … yes, I can hear you." I tried to sit up as he held me.

"Easy, honey."

"What happened? Did you find Mandy?"

He looked at me with complete shock. "What?"

"Did you find Mandy, Jim?" He smiled while pushing my hair out of my eyes.

"No, my love. She'll be here in the morning." I kissed his hand, and then he helped me get to my feet.

We walked arm-in-arm back to the house. Layla soon ran up behind us. She looked at me, and I knelt, looked her in the eye, and said, "There's my sweet girl. I've missed you so much!" Her tailed seemed to wag her entire body, as she then realized I was back. She hugged me in her own special way. It brought tears to my eyes. Jim fought back tears as well.

Back at the house, we walked into our bedroom. I sat on the window seat to remove my shoes as Jim walked in with the first aid kit to assist me in cleaning up my scrapes. I pulled my left knee up to rest on the seat. "Boy, I really did it this time didn't I, baby?"

Jim knelt as he lay his head on my knees. "No, sweetheart. We're just fine."

I looked out the window. Nothing really caught my attention. I just gazed out the window, trying to understand where the time had gone, and how much of it. I lost my thoughts in the thievery of this disease, and how it shamelessly robbed me of my mind, my body, and most of all…my family. Jim leaned back for a moment and said, "That's it."

I turned to him, "What?" I asked.

He answered, "You, gazing out the window, the painting, Mandy."

*Yes,* I thought, *of course. Now I understand. That's why I can't recall another family, that's why I can't remember Beth Ann. I'm Beth Ann! Jim is my husband, Amanda is our daughter ...*

I felt my necklace, the same as my daughter's. I knew all at once who I was, what I was suffering from. I knew then how limited my time with Jim and my family would be. Jim leaned down, pulling my chin up to meet his stare. Our souls melted together. I wanted to remember the moment our eyes locked into that implausible moment in time together even more, the moment we both would reach the point of no return. The moment when we both knew we belonged completely to each other and no one else mattered.

# CHAPTER 12
## I am Beth Ann Dean

I awoke to the sound of birds chirping outside the window. I sat up, tied my hair in a makeshift knot, wrapped myself in a sheet, and walked into the kitchen. The fresh-brewed coffee aroma lingered. Layla was barking in the distance, Jim chuckling and offering her grunted commands in a joyous tone.

"Go get it, girl, Layla, atta girl!" As Layla came running back to him, Jim knelt to scratch her head and take the stick back for another throw. "Good girl, Layla, what a good girl!" Layla's tail wagged as she impatiently waited for Jim to throw the stick again.

She didn't have to wait long.

*They seem so happy*, I silently observed. I wandered into the kitchen for the hot liquid energy I needed so desperately. Sipping from my cup, I went to the window. Jim and Layla were frolicking and playing on the far side of the garden. Jim could barely grab and fling the little stick fast enough before Layla bounded at it. I just stood there watching, chuckling into my cup, reminding myself not take such moments for granted. And as much as I was tempted to join in on the fun, I decided to stay back and allow the two of them their joyful time together. For a moment, I nearly forgot my disease. I was truly happy.

A few lone tears crept down my cheeks.

*If only ...*

Smiling through the tears while listening intently to Jim's carefree laughter, the wave of their life's memories warmed me, body and soul. I drifted off to memories of the day we met, that life-changing moment when I first laid eyes on Jim; that new, crazed flurry in my stomach was still there every time I looked at him, at the inescapable glisten in his eyes. The rush of memories flashed through my mind: All the joy we'd shared, the devotion, heartbreak, the rare yet heated arguments, our undeniable infatuation with each other, and the sweetest and most tender moments. And they took the shape of Jim himself, a masculine, glowing personality I just couldn't take my eyes off of. I felt my cheeks quivering, my eyesight fogged with tears, one for each precious memory as they all slowly slipped away.

"Good morning, Sunshine!" he cheerfully blurted. He greeted me with a tender kiss on the forehead and a glass of freshly squeezed orange juice. "You look rested. Mandy will be here in about an hour."

I sat down at the kitchen table. "She's coming all the way out here?"

He finished making breakfast. "Coming in for a long weekend."

I turned around to soak in all the memories of this beautiful home we'd made. I looked at Jim to see him smile, as if no one was watching. He was so completely happy in that moment. I loved listening to him humming in the kitchen, breathing in the delicious smell of cinnamon French toast. I loved gazing at the olive trees gently swaying in the breeze, and feeling the cool breeze flowing in through the top of the back door. We had an old world Dutch door which we used to open only the top portion of so we could enjoy the freshness of the outdoor air while not having to worry with the little ones getting out. I could almost hear the giggles and laughter of children chasing Layla and *vice versa*.

"Beth Ann?" Jim asked. "Beth Ann? Honey?" he urged. Clearing my throat, I answered, "Yes, sweetheart. I'm fine.

Let me go throw on some clothes. Be right back." He turned around and walked to the stove.

We sat in the kitchen and finished breakfast.

Jim leaned over and grabbed my hand. "How would you like to take a trip?"

"Trip?"

"We always go to *N'awlins* for Halloween. So, what do you think?"

In wide-eyed excitement, I shrieked, "*Nola*? I'd love that!"

His grin widened. "I thought you would. I've already confirmed us for the Halloween party at Ted and Sam's as well."

A flood of memories flash through my mind: The two people in the photo next to the bookcase. *That's Ted and Sam ... Samantha, has to be!* "How much fun would that be?"

Jim continued, "We could stay at our favorite hotel in the French Quarter and do the Halloween crawl."

I jumped up to hug his neck, "Oh honey, that sounds amazing! Can we order in our favorite PB&Js?" His eyes twinkled as he placed me sweetly on his lap. "And we could stay a night or two with Ted and Sam?"

Jim pulled my chin down to peck me on the lips. "Absolutely." I gazed deeply into his eyes, cradled his face in my hands, kissed his forehead, and whispered, "I love you." He nuzzled the side of his face onto my chest. "And I love you." We savored the moment just sitting there together, holding each other.

The wave of memories indeed hit me hard. I realized that we had spent many seasons in New Orleans. I remembered how much fun we had on our trips there. There is no place quite like New Orleans at Halloween. Our favorite hotel was located on the tip of the French Quarter. It hadn't been nicknamed *The Belle of New Orleans* for nothing. It was adorned with lush furnishings, as the hotel dated back to 1907. Remembering the history of this hotel alone was enough to send shivers up and down my spine, as it has been reported to be one of the most haunted hotels in all of New Orleans. We had a lot of friends who had joined us there quite a few years running, and we always had the most amazing time. Ted and Sam's historic mansion was nothing short of spectacular, and their parties were larger-than-life. It was at that very moment that I remembered what my ankle tattoo meant. Lizzie confidently brushed her hair back and nudged me, *Oh darling, we are going to have one hell of a good time!* I didn't fight her, because I knew she was absolutely on point. And I was ready.

Even with my scattered memory, I had an innate compulsion to go to New Orleans. I'd always enjoyed Halloween as a kid, the color and the costumes, the scary fun. It only occurred to me then how scary life could really be, and how important it was to be able to face that fright, to reduce it to something manageable, something funny and harmless. I wondered how and why all the fear should be marbled into my sex life, but all at once I was overwhelmed with the complexity of it, the unanswerable questions. I had a hard enough time not getting lost in a corn maze to bother with the Freudian aspects of my sex life. I liked it. I couldn't identify or describe it, but there was something in me screaming out, *Yes, let's go and let's go now!*

I stood myself up from Jim's lap while facing him. I pulled his chin up to focus on me as I ran my fingers through his hair. Brushing my finger across his lower lip, I caught his eyes with mine. "We are going to have the best Halloween yet."

He kissed my finger with a slow, sly grin. "There you

are." He pulled me close while he nuzzled my breasts once more in response. He stood as my eyes followed. He glanced past me for a moment, then backed up. He moved in to trace the outline of my neck with his finger. "Best Halloween yet, huh?" he taunted. My lips parted for a moment as I prepared to answer him, but he shushed me abruptly with his finger. "Just show me."

# CHAPTER 13
## Amanda

"Hello-*ooo*?" The sweet, angelic voice wafted in from the front door. "Hello? Anyone home?" The voice got louder as its source came closer. We both snapped back to our reality as my eyes widened. My heart beat faster. I was frozen with fear. Jim's look softened as he observed me, mouthing, *It's okay.* My lower lip trembled as I turned to see the golden-haired beauty stepping into the doorway. She turned to me, placing her hand over her mouth, as she struggled back her tears. My mouth was agape as our eyes met, a loud gasp was my best attempt at keeping my composure. I was drawn to her. We each took a step, and finally she hurried to me while sniveling inaudibly in this soft and tender voice.

She wrapped her arms around me. "*Mooommmm!*" Elated tears streamed down my cheeks. Nothing could have prepared me for seeing her after what seemed to be an entire lifespan. It all seemed to come down to that single moment. I cradled her head in my hands, pulling her tight, the sweet honeysuckle scent of her hair filling my nostrils. Mandy dabbed the tears from her cheeks as she looked over to Jim, who was every bit expressive as we were. She pulled him in, and the three of us stood there hugging. It was more than I could fully comprehend, no room for words, thoughts, doubts.

Jim pulled himself away. "Hey Mandy, are you hungry?"

She giggled. "I'm starving, Daddy!" I excused myself to the bathroom as the two of them headed to the kitchen.

I closed the bathroom door, looked into the mirror, and erupted into tears. *Where have I been? Where have I been staying, who's been taking care of me? Mandy? Jim? Did I wander away from some hospital somewhere, or worse, an asylum of some kind?*

I splashed water on my face. Catching the reflection of my necklace in the mirror, I stared down to study it closely, a ruby heart mounted in white gold. I dried my face with the towel and sauntered out into the hallway toward the painting.

There she was, my precious ballerina. She had the most beautiful long golden hair. Her alabaster skin was glowing, and I recognized that familiar gaze Jim spoke with me about. She had the same pendant around her neck that I did, and I reached for mine. *How beautiful she is, how sad. What could possibly have made this sweet angelic girl so fearful? What must have been going through her mind?*

Warm arms wrapped around my waist from the back. "Twin hearts," Mandy whispered as she reached for her pendant. I faced her. "I love you, Mommy."

All of a sudden I wasn't looking at this lovely young woman but my little girl, banana-mush face, smacking her baby spoon on the tray of her high chair in an effort to pull my attention away from the sink and the dishes. Her pint-sized blonde pig-tails made her downright adorable. Banging on the bottom of her banana bowl, trying to speak or sing or scream or all at once. She was a lovable mess.

Jim had just come in through the front door, years earlier, our infant daughter shrieking with glee in my memory.

He was wearing the jeans I loved to see him in, and he knew I loved it. They just seemed to worship his body. Mandy's legs and arms paddled and paddled even more anxiously. *Daa-daa!* she'd blurted out.

*Her first word!* Even baby Amanda seemed surprised.

Jim bolted to her high chair. She blinked those beautiful long eyelashes and giggled proudly as she offered him gigantic wet banana kisses. Jim showered her with praise and kisses as well. She continued those tickle-your-soul giggles with dimples a mile wide.

My mind flashed to a moment after putting the jubilant child to bed for a nap.

Jim had begun kissing the back of my neck, goosebumps rose all over my back. He'd run his hand down, around, and then up into the front slit of my cut-off jean shorts. They were so short the front pockets hung down below the cut, but I knew that was the way he enjoyed them. The heat of his breath had made it impossible to hide the hardness of my nipples through this fitted white razorback shirt, and the trail of goosebumps traveling down my bronzed legs.

I raised my arms up behind my neck to cradle his, knowing there was just enough soapy warm water in my hands to easily run down my arms and splash onto my shirt. I knew how much it enticed him when I paraded around the house in little to no clothes. I had been waiting for this greeting all day. His right hand traced the front fray of my cutoff shorts, as his other hand probed under my wet shirt and up to my fully erect nipple. He fondled and squeezed my nipple while kissing my neck. I tugged his ear down to my mouth and whispered, "Oh, yes. Daddy's home."

But Amanda's voice snapped me back to the present, shattering my lusty recollection.

"Mom, let's just be grateful we are together and appreciate every moment, okay?" she requested, with those remarkable dove-like eyes and beautifully long lashes. I pulled her tight, smelling her hair once more. "Oh yes, my love. Oh yes." Struggling to regain my composure, I insisted, "Okay, now go eat!" She turned toward the kitchen, as I playfully swatted her butt.

She yelped. "Some things never change around here!" We both giggled in unison as I watched her practically skip into the kitchen to join Jim.

The three of us sat around the table, not far from where her high chair had been many years ago. Neither Jim nor I were hungry, but we both nibbled a bit to keep Mandy company. Sipping my coffee, I looked down at her flip-flops. "Honey, aren't your feet cold?"

"Not at all. Are yours?"

I was wearing flip-flops too, the small tattoo on the outside of my left ankle peeking out. It was very small. I took a closer look while the two of them carried on a conversation. I pulled my ankle back to examine it further.

The red tattoo, about an inch around, featured *VE* in scripted letters. I quietly lowered my foot and went back to my coffee. Jim looked at me and slowly winked.

"So, kids," Mandy said with a smiling irony, "I'm supposed to meet Kendall tomorrow evening. What time are we heading out tomorrow?"

"I'm sorry, what?"

Jim said to me, "I already have everything packed, my love. We'll be wheels up around noon. So let's leave here by ten."

*Wait,* I wondered, *where are we going? What's going on now?*

Mandy asked me, "Mom, are you okay?"

Painfully and consciously aware of my fading, I answered, "Yes, sweetheart, it was just a big day today. I think I'm going to go lie down for a bit."

Jim said, "I'll come lie down with you."

*

"*Yooo-hoooo*, wake up, sleepy heads," chirped young Amanda. "We need to leave in a couple hours, and Carl just called to confirm our takeoff time."

I pulled down the sheet, which had made its way over my

face, sat up in our bed and looked at Jim. He was still lying on his stomach with his pillow over his head. He liked sleeping without a shirt, which allowed me to caress the warmth of his shoulder while leaning over to kiss the back of his neck. "Hey sleepy," I whispered. He whimpered a bit, but still hadn't moved. "Time to get up, my love," I continued.

He inhaled deeply as he pulled his head out from under his pillow and squinted. "Mornin', baby."

I was peaked with excitement, my blood tingling. I'd come to grips with who I was, not Lizzie or Liz but Beth Ann Dean, wife and mother. I had a cognitive disease, and that was going to be a problem for me, a big one.

But I was alive and in love and we were off to enjoy our time together, our friends, ourselves and each other. I knew who I was and I knew where I was going, and though most people might have taken that for granted, I was relishing every bit of it.

Jim stretched and yawned as we both pulled ourselves from our soft and fluffy oasis. "Coffee smells good!" he bellowed out the bedroom door to Mandy as he made his way to the bathroom.

"Thanks, Dad," Amanda echoed from the kitchen.

# CHAPTER 14
## *Nola*

"Good morning, Captain Carl," Jim greeted with a great big smile and salute as he stepped on board.

"Good morning, sir," Carl answered, returning the salute. The two of them shook hands. "Weather looks good into New Orleans, so it looks like we're in for a smooth ride today, sunshine and clear skies," he continued.

"Oh yes. Just what I like to hear," Jim responded.

Amanda and I stepped in to give Carl a quick hug and greeting, making our way to our chairs. "I truly hate flying," she said, grabbing a bottle of water and plopping down in her chair. Jim and I looked at each other. I smiled and he rolled his eyes.

"You could always walk," Jim said with a little smile.

Amanda smirked sheepishly and placed her earbuds in her ears. We both shook our heads. Amanda looked at me and mouthed, *Sorry.* Pulling down her window shade, I could hear Jane Jensen's "Fly Home" playing through her ear buds. Good to know she hadn't lost her good taste in music.

*

The tires squealed as we felt the bounce upon landing. The sun was shining and it was hot and humid. Mandy smiled relieved, removed her earbuds, and fiercely began texting, and that was all we saw of her face for another hour.

We loaded into the car, pulled down the top, and drove into the Big Easy. I yanked the Chicago Cubs baseball cap off my head for the first time since I got on the plane. I slung my foot up over the passenger door, Bo Hica blasting on the stereo. All three of us were in our element; the freedom of the road, the wind blowing through our hair, the sweet sounding music playing, and the laughter of the three of us merely enjoying the moment together.

We pulled up to the front of Kendall's home. Amanda yelped as she practically leapt out of the car to greet Kendall at the door. Seeing the old friends reunited, Beth Ann was struck by memories that neither Liz nor Lizzie could touch: Hours playing in the park, the shriek of Christmas mornings, the gut-wrenching tears of teenage heartbreak. Beth Ann had lived it all with her family, she could now recall in clearer and clearer detail. And though Amanda and her friend were in their first few years of college, they seemed to be the young girls of bygone years, happier and more carefree times.

Amanda quickly returned to grab her bag from the back, waving goodbye, and ran to Kendall's walkway. They were interlocked tightly. Kendall's mother walked up from inside the house.

Kendall's mother, Lenore, and I both knew how much the girls had missed each other, and didn't want to waste a single moment on small-talk when the girls could spend much-needed quality time together. We both waved back and Jim pulled away from the house.

Jim said, "You're all mine now, baby," and we sped away.

I wasn't sure if it was the sultry air or the warmth of the sun which seemed to calm my spirit, but both were inviting and most welcomed. I threw my head back, hair flying in the breeze.

We made our way to the outskirts of the French Quarter, just beyond the Garden District.

*

Downtown New Orleans was a wry combination of the city's historic past and of its contemporary present. Sleek glass office buildings rose up around the French wrought iron balconies which just screamed for some colorfully dressed women, flaunting their wares for passing sailors.

But there were parts that seemed just like Downtown Anywhere, U.S.A. with homeless men and women shambling, police cars rolling by, streetlights and crosswalks and shiny sedans parked under the old-fashioned gaslights.

The world's oldest streetcar lanes took us farther into the famed Garden District, a distinct area of one of the most distinct towns in all the world.

New Orleans's Garden District was and remains a beckoning to the faded glories of the Old South. Grassy esplanades separated the streets into pairs of one-way lanes, trees lining the sidewalks casting bucolic shade as the sun went down. The sky bled orange and red and yellow and purple in an almost supernatural aura above us.

Grand homes passed by on either side, the mansions of bygone millionaires, once the city's elite and still a significant cut above the grime and grim realities of the Big Easy. Even the history those magnificent homes represented was soiled with the blemish of hatred, fear, slavery, death. The dark spirits of those who suffered seemed to hover around that place, lurking in the shadows, filling the place with a grave sense of finality. I couldn't ignore the feeling that something big was going to happen, that we were getting closer and closer to more than just a party. This was a town of secrets and shame, of sin and degradation. Those things were at the heart of my quandary, I knew, but they were powerful demons to face.

I smiled at Jim and he smiled back.

*At least I won't have to face them alone ... I hope.*

But my doubts about Jim didn't last long, they never could. I knew I was his wife and I knew he loved me. He wasn't going to let anything bad happen to me, and he surely wasn't there to orchestrate any evil against me.

*But what if they've tricked him,* I couldn't help but wonder, *or brainwashed him? Maybe they're drugging all the food, so Jim's poisoning both of us without even realizing? Can it be that we're both being duped, that it's a double sacrifice of some kind, something even Jim couldn't have anticipated?*

We pulled in to one of the most dramatic driveways in all of historic New Orleans. Ted and Sam left nothing to the imagination when they underwent this tremendous renovation and fully restored this quintessential French Creole colonial mansion. The estate had been passed on to Ted and Sam immediately following their nuptials. Servants' quarters, stables, and a very rare French Creole barn surrounded the sprawling estate, secluded quietly away from all the hustle and bustle of town. The quarter-mile drive from the main road led us down the impeccably landscaped greenery, and Crepe Myrtle-lined driveway, up to the towering wrought iron gates which welcomed us. The gates swung open wide and we drove in. I was nervous, conflicted, filled with anticipation and energy but unable to ignore that creeping sensation in the back of my brain that warned me: I was passing a point of no return.

The gates closed behind us.

# CHAPTER 15
## Ted and Sam

The chill of the autumn breeze whistled beneath the brittle, dancing leaves. We turned the corner of the cobblestone driveway to pull up to the front of the main house, when all I could do was gasp at its majestic beauty. This three-story masterpiece was adorned with wrought iron balconies and French doors. We pulled to a stop.

"*Oooohhhh*, Ted! Honey, they're *heeeeere!*" Sam yelled as she ran straight from the front door to greet us. Jim laughed as he saw her running from the door, down the steps to the car.

They looked just as they did in the photo back at the house, and that only inspired returns of the flashes in my memory, the two costumed figures in the basement.

Jim stopped the car and I jumped out. "Samantha, I've missed you so much." I hugged her as though my life depended on it. The familiar fragrance of her long brown hair, bouncing around her shoulders. Suddenly we were college roommates once more, with not a care in the world. I closed my eyes tightly, to hold on as long as possible.

Ted's black hair and dark eyes remained as clear and crisp as his olive complexion. "Oh my God, Beth Ann!" Ted exclaimed. "Come to Teddy Bear." He chuckled, arms open wide. Armed with my sheepish grin and the dimples Ted always seemed to love, I practically swooned, falling deeply into his arms. The smell of his cologne always did make my knees buckle. And yet he never would tell me the name of it. He rubbed his hand down my hair, guiding my face up gently as he delicately kissed my nose. "I've missed you, Bethie," he whispered.

I tiptoed up to kiss his cheek, answering, "I missed you too." Jim walked up behind me as Ted broke away to greet him. "You'd think with having your own plane that coming to visit wouldn't be that big a deal, huh?" They hugged that brotherly hug that only true friends could. The four of us walked arm-in-arm inside their home.

Jim gasped, as he stood in the grand foyer. They had been consumed with their remodel efforts for a couple years now, and the results took our breath away. Their biggest concern was to preserve all the ornate architectural details from this old world relic, and fine-tune it to their personal style and luxury standards of today.

They'd nailed it.

The twelve-foot soaring ceilings, crown molding, original medallions, and *gasoliers* were spectacular. Jim stroked and studied the matchless detail of the trim woodwork. He and Ted started chatting about the detail, the craftsmanship, then drifted out of the room, lost in their own conversation.

Sam looked me up and down as we carried the bags up the stairs. "Oh my gosh babe, you're gettin' so skinny. We're gonna have to feed you good!" Sam's southern drawl echoed as we climbed the stairs. At the top of the stairs, Sam sighed and set Jim's bag down.

"You okay?"

"Yes, sweetheart, I'm fine." I touched her cheek as she nuzzled my hand with her shoulder.

"We've missed you guys so much," she went on, as her eyes began to twinkle a bit.

"We're so happy to be here."

Walking down the hallway, I was almost transfixed by the antique fixtures, exposed brick, magnificent tapestries. The stories we used to tell of all the goings-on in this place sent chills up my spine. However, this eighteenth century landmark was undeniably a French archetypical masterpiece. On the way in, it was easy to appreciate the grandeur of this stately mansion. The interior had been completely remodeled and exquisitely refined. The parlor lay through the finely crafted French doors to the right of the grand foyer. Just beyond the parlor lay the formal living and dining rooms, sun streaming in through the leaded-glass windows. The main kitchen featured soapstone counter tops, deep oak cabinets, and a light-filled keeping room adjacent to a large sit-in bay window. The wine cellar sat just below the kitchen, and the elevator would move us down to the wine cellar or up to the second and third floors with ease. The dumbwaiter was fully functional as well. I chuckled to recall one of our drunken weight experiments of years past.

We stopped at a set of exquisite French doors at the end of the left hallway. "We hope you'll both be very … *comfortable* here." I gasped as I stepped over the threshold into this enchanted French *boudoir*.

The walls were color washed with a faux texture finish in deep burgundy. A fabric-draped accent wall stood boldly behind a huge four-poster king-sized. To the left of the bed were two exquisite ornate Baroque mahogany chairs with lush upholstery in deep velvet, a highboy dresser, and a vanity table coupled with an elegant Victorian settee with a tufted back. The heavy maroon drapery panels hung from cciling to floor and were pulled back graciously with long-hanging tassels. The cabaret-style table lamps with sheer fabric shades cast dimmed lighting throughout the boudoir, countering a fire roaring in the fireplace.

Sam traced my lips with her eyes, her own lips parting. Her mischievous eyes made my whole body tingle. It was all coming back to me. Sam's hand moved up to my face, she touched my lips with her finger, she leaned in to kiss me. Sam was so sweet and gentle at first that it tickled me. Her soft tongue swept across my lip, as I slowly met her tongue with mine. She pulled back and sighed. "We have a very big evening planned, my darling. Best get ready." Glancing my shoulder with the tips of her fingers, she left.

I stood alone, remembering just how close our friendship really was. Sam and I shared a certain fondness for each other, one that our husbands didn't seem to mind at all. In fact, there had been many times, as I thought about it, when the four of us enjoyed each other all at once. Generally it was just me and Sam, as Jim and Ted were happy enough just to watch.

I sat down on the bed, remembering the tenderness of our relationship, as I moved my hand down to caress my wetness. Leaning back and pushing my hand down the front of my jeans, I moaned as the pressure started to build. I fingered and pulsed until the heat flashed through my body. The softer my fingers pulsated the wetter I became. I shimmied out of my jeans and spread my legs wider. The soft motion sent a fiery hot rush shooting through my veins, as I cried out with sweet release. My racing heart finally slowed as I rolled over.

I walked down the dark hallway toward the sound of Jim and Teddy talking by the fireplace, over a scotch. Jim's back was facing me so he didn't hear my approach. Sam was getting ready upstairs. The sound of classical music filled the room.

"Amanda? She's fine, Ted, fine. Why do you ask?"

"Oh, um, nothing, really, I know things got a little difficult around the house … "

"It's happening again," Jim said. "I made a commitment to her. I love her, Teddy."

"Jim, I know Beth Ann. I've known her most of my adult life, and I know her well enough to know that she would understand if you just walked away from all this."

"No, Teddy, no! I took a vow! After all she has given me and continues to do for me? I would never … we're in this together, Ted," Jim circled his finger on the rim of his glass. "A little piece of my heart breaks every time she leaves me. And then … it grows back even stronger every time she comes back." He stood and walked toward the fireplace. "Our life is us together, nothing else. It doesn't matter how we manage, as long as we stay together. This woman is my wife, my life, my whole heart. She trusts me."

Clearing his throat slightly, Teddy looked to Jim. "And she would do the same for you. Her whole world is you. As much as Sam and I love each other? We know we can only aspire to have half the love the two of you have."

I smiled and turned away, glad to hear these reassuring words. But there was something I just couldn't figure out about Ted and Sam. *Were they the two people I was with in my basement?* I felt like they had the key somehow, the answer to the puzzle I was trying to solve: *Where was I going that morning, when I woke up in the car on the side of the road? It has something to do with Ted and Sam … and … and Mandy?*

I rubbed my temple, the very idea that my daughter would be wrapped up in something she didn't fully understand, which I didn't entirely understand, was overwhelming for me.

But I was quick to calm myself. *Mandy's safe with her friend, Jim and I can handle these people, whatever they have in mind. No reason to make any assumptions, jump to any conclusions. This is all in good fun.*

*Isn't it?*

# CHAPTER 16
## Halloween

I'd been very excited about the party. Being with Ted and Sam again gave me a warmth I hadn't found with any other pair, and the thrill of the trip and the exotic surroundings were hard to ignore. I almost felt that little spark of Lizzie deep down inside me, wanting to come out and play.

But I knew I couldn't just relinquish myself to my baser self yet again. I'd done it before, and I knew that's why Jim and I had come to New Orleans in the first place, to partake in the magic and mystery and spectacle. But there was a price to be paid for all that pleasure, I was sure of it. And more and more I became concerned that the time to collect had arrived.

Jim and I pulled the masks over our faces to fit in with the others. I wore the mask I was handed, a pretty woman's face with tiny lips and nose, big eyes, almost alien in her featureless face. Jim's mask was a skull, a barebones grin of wicked dominion. With his thick black robe, he was the visage of death itself.

And I was glad. I was nervous, and I wanted no less than such an intimidating partner. I knew I was facing more than a simple romp, even more than a complex orgy as we'd had before. There was more to this group than it appeared, and the higher up the spiral of power and influence went, the vaguer and indistinct it was. Who were they? What did they want from me? They wanted more from me than just my body, more even than my silence or my soul.

And the time had come for them to collect. I felt it in my bones, a sense of foreboding, looming danger. I wasn't sure if it was just that we were in such a fabled land as New Orleans, with its history of zombies and the black arts, especially on Halloween of all nights.

But I also knew somehow, knowing without knowing, that the seasons had power, that certain days were ordained with energies that could be harvested, for good or for ill. And that night was imbued with a vibration that I could feel as surely as I could feel the humid breeze on my skin.

I was half-ready to chalk it up to my disease, knowing I couldn't entirely trust myself to decipher the truth from reality, and that made it all the more frightening. I wouldn't have minded facing any enemy, as long as I knew what that enemy was and what it wanted. Instead my future loomed in the shadows, hidden and ready to pounce.

Whatever was waiting for us, I wanted and needed Jim by my side. *Let them be intimidated by him,* I felt, *let them get the idea that, if they tangle with me, they may have to deal with the Grim Reaper himself, in more ways than just the figurative. Because I know Jim will kill for me if he has to, die for me if he has to.*

And both were not only possible, but they seemed increasingly likely.

Everybody was in costume, though this was no mere gaggle of superheroes and historical figures. Everybody wore masks.

Mardi Gras masks were everywhere, metallic colors intricately detailed with tiny jewels and great, long feathers stretching out on each side. Gorgeous women seemed to have stepped out of time, from an Elizabethan corridor where Victorian modesty had given way to perverse sexuality. They wore spangled unitards, studded and bejeweled, clinging to their lean and well-toned bodies, breasts and hips and flanks and thighs in full display. When I looked more closely at one young woman, I saw that she was actually naked and had been painted from head to toe in metallic paint, a living silver statue.

A woman in one corner of the room was entirely decked out in leather; studded cap and vest, tight leather bikini trunks, spiked leather wristband. My eyes followed the leash in her hand to the man on the other end, on all fours like a dog, completely bare-assed naked, the leash attached to a collar around his neck.

And there were others who wore thick red robes, some of their masks garish and ugly. Goats with horns and downturned brows, sheep with bulging, frightened eyes, lion and bear and tiger. But animals of the natural world were only a suggestion of what they'd find farther into the crowd: The faces of reptile creatures, hybrids of human and amphibian, the golden horns of mythical unicorns and dragons. Some young women drifted by in green silk robes, languid against their lithe limbs, cats' eyes peering out from behind green masks as those spirits of the glade flittered and fluttered.

I thought I saw huge, colorful wings on women in skintight spangling black unitards, arms folded in against their lean bodies to complete the effect.

I felt like I suddenly understood myself just a bit better, as if being there in New Orleans had contributed another piece of the puzzle that was Beth Ann Dean. In that dreamy environment, everybody fantastical, there was no reality. There, I didn't need to remember my own name, I didn't need to find my way home. There were no names to remember, no homes to go to.

A string quartet played from a corner of the packed, palatial living room, cello low and deep, viola sad and stirring, violin sharp and playful, vibrato wafting above the crowd. Incense filled the air, heavy and oaky, burning my nostrils as it curled in the back of my head. I almost felt like it had some intoxicating quality, opiated somehow, but I couldn't be sure.

I couldn't entirely trust myself or my senses or my memory. It made things all the more difficult, and all the more urgent. I felt like I was getting closer and closer with every step. But I also knew I was getting in deeper and deeper; deeper into my past, my own secrets and the secrets being kept from me.

Ted and Sam approached us. Though they were covered head-to-toe with animal masks and hide-like robes, he a jackal and she a cheetah, I knew right away who they were. *How am I able to identify their bodies through the capes, through the masks?*

But there was little time to think about it and no time to think about everything else that was commanding my attention. Ted and Sam turned, and both Jim and I knew we should follow. We'd only been through half the house, after all, and this was a mansion from another time, with secrets burying secrets encircling puzzles wrapped in riddles.

But one riddle unwound before my mind's eye, and with a return of those fleeting visuals of the two costumed figures in the basement. They had definitely been Ted and Sam, their hands all over me, ravaging me.

The mansion's rooms were small, as rooms were in the century of their construction. And they felt even smaller with the massive crowd, the hum of their muttered conversations beneath their masks, music creeping around between the guests, jammed together in a cloud of perfume, cologne, cigarette smoke, opium, hash, pot, cigars, brandy, body odor, regret, corruption, shame, rot.

I tried to be careful to watch my mind and where it may take me. I had to remain in control. Lizzie could not be allowed to take control in this situation, or else I may be lost to her forever, never able to fully control myself. Lizzie was Liz's problem, after all.

*But if I'm ever going to get out of here alive,* I told myself with grave certainty, *never mind discover what I'm truly doing here in the first place, if I don't remember one thing above all others:*

*I am Beth Ann Dean.*

And despite my costume, I couldn't help imagining that everybody there knew who I was. They knew my circumstances. They'd been expecting me, it seemed. They were ready.

They had plans of their own.

I felt like I'd known their plan at some point, whatever it was. I knew my disease was preventing me from recalling, from drawing out that final piece to the puzzle. But I felt like I was getting closer to an answer, closer with every step. They accepted me and Jim as two of their own. But I couldn't help wonder, *Why? What part am I expected to play in all this?*

Ted and Sam led us into the yard, a stately porch leading down to a lovely garden, thick with statues and fountains, cypress trees, potted plants, iguana looking down from the beams, big eyes bugging, heads turning in constant confusion.

I knew just how they felt.

Ted and Sam led us across the yard without making a sound, others glancing at them from behind their various masks, looking at one another in silent concern, then back at me and Jim. Whatever they knew, they weren't sharing it.

Ted and Sam led us to an old stone crypt, tall, marble, a statue of St. James staring into the distance in a silent herald of terrible things to come.

Ted and Sam looked at each other, then at us. We shared a quiet confirmation before Ted and Sam turned to push the stone door of the little mausoleum open. For a slab of such considerable weight, the door glided open with frightening ease. Ted and Sam stepped back and Ted held his hand out, gesturing toward the opened doorway. They waited. Jim and I knew what we had to do, where we had to go, though I still wasn't sure why.

My heart was pounding as I stepped into the stone chamber, sudden claustrophobia shaking my soul. As always, Jim read my mind, my body, my soul. His hand took mine, pumping in his calming strength, his silent reassurance as we stepped deeper into that musky cavern.

It reminded me at once of the secret basement in our home, a place of dark secrets, dimly it, threatening. That stone slab closed behind us and we were plunged into utter darkness, complete and airless and potentially deadly. *We could be trapped in here,* it struck me. *I've got to get out now!*

Jim felt me panic and squeezed my hand. His calming presence was the only thing preventing my terrified scream. Soon enough, a torch lit up, revealing a glowing orb. Ted held the torch to light up the narrow little stone cavern. Ted and Sam led me and Jim forward, deeper into whatever nightmare awaited us. I looked back, the corridor unlit behind us.

There was no going back.

So I walked with Jim down that strange rabbit hole, knowing somehow that I was leaving everything in my life behind, once and for all. It was more than a strange place, unexplained by the landscape on the surface above it. I felt as if I was living my own disease, gradually sinking deeper into a world of confusion, a morass to trap me, lock me in, pull me down, finally going under …

I gasped and clutched Jim's hand as we reached the end of the corridor. Another stone slab like the first one opened in Ted's hand and he and Sam led us into another yard, not too different from the first. I looked around to see the high hedges all around the property, hints of stone wall behind them.

*Must be the place on the next street over, the house behind Ted and Sam's,* I reasoned. *Do they own both? Or is this the house of the true masters of the local chapter? Are these people so secretive and powerful that they need Sam and Ted to cover for them, one massive step further removed from the populace? Who are these people that they need so much anonymity? And what are they doing that they need so much protection from?*

*No,* I realized, remembering without remembering, *these people are more powerful than Ted and Sam, yes. They brought Ted and Sam into this society, just as Ted and Sam brought me in! That's right! And Jim ... Jim ... Jim never cared much for it? He's just here for me.*

*But ... why am I here?*

*And if the people who own this house are Ted and Sam's superiors, they're surely not the top of the power pyramid, they can't be!* The vibrations were powerful in that yard, even more so than in the other property; darker, more sinister.

*No, that's your imagination,* I cautioned myself. *Don't get carried away! Stay sharp, look alive ... while you still can!*

This yard was behind a similar house, filled with like-robed guests in crude masks, long toothy snouts of faux hogs and oxen. Ted and Sam led us through a maze-like garden, potted plants rising up to lead them closer to the center of the yard. There toward the center the various paths led to a broader, empty space with a stone slab in the center. I knew instantly that it was an altar, a sarcophagus, a plate to serve up some pure, wanton soul to the powers that be and many that aren't.

Drums leaked in from the background, I wasn't even sure from where. I was distracted by the several golden cages, six feet high, with naked women dancing to the steady beat. They swayed their hips, their unclothed bodies covered in solid-colored paint; one woman gold from head to toe, one silver, one bright red, one completely white.

I stuck closer to Jim. I couldn't help but wonder, *Is that stone slab for me? Is that why Ted and Sam invited us here, to lure me into a trap? And what about Jim?* I squeezed his hand tighter and I felt his warmth, his strength, his purity.

*No, not Jim; he's with me no matter what. I know that. But that's all I know.*

I looked around, counting at least a hundred people cluttered in those winding paths around us, leading to the center of the yard. Instead of wondering what they were planning, I was wondering how long we'd manage to fight them off, how far we'd get before they'd bear down on us, overwhelming us by sheer numbers, to drag us to our terrible deaths.

This is what I was up against, I realized, still not sure of exactly what that meant. But I knew this cabal went straight back to everything that had been troubling me, what I'd been striving to achieve.

Or destroy.

I knew somehow that I was in over my head, that whatever evil I was there to face down would ultimately be beyond my reach. But there was something I could do, some purpose for my presence there, and I was bound to discover it and then fulfill it.

Fate clung to the mist.

I knew there was some matter of timing, a predestined event, a prophecy that somehow involved me. But I also felt somehow that those energies could be turned against those who sought to manipulate them and me. Whatever had been meant for my harm could be used for my benefit, my enemy's strengths could always be turned into vulnerabilities.

And so could my own.

The key was to knowing which was which, but that would be almost impossible.

The drums got louder, steady, gradually increasing in almost imperceptible increments. A low chant rose up to underscore that pulsing percussion, each making the other louder and louder. The chant was no word but a grunt, a vague, *"Har-umph,"* which they repeated endlessly.

The women in the cages danced with greater fury, grabbing the bars of their cages and pulling, yanking fruitlessly to free themselves, shaking their long, dyed hair, cocking their painted hips and hairless loins.

Other women danced around the altar, flowing silk robes with slits up the sides, translucent in the moonlight, breasts high and proud, even their hardened nipples visible, their excitement growing with every step, every thump of the drum, the chant rising up to consume us all.

Louder and louder, faster and faster, the sound and the crowd was closing in on us, deliberate, purposeful. Thump and chant, louder and louder, and Jim and I could only cling to one another until the cacophony reached a fever pitch.

The crowd all turned away from us to the stone doorway which was the only way back into the secret passageway, the object of the evening's purpose was at last introduced.

My heart almost stopped in my chest.

# CHAPTER 17
## Revelations

My spine stiffened as the crowd parted, the drums pounding louder, the chanting not abating as several masked men walked toward the altar. It took me a moment or two before I could make out the figure of the girl in their center. I knew right away it was a girl by the shape of her frame, slender under her white silk robe.

Her hair was tied back and tucked under her full-head mask of a young maiden, with a featureless face like my own mask, a long golden wig cascading from the back. They dragged her with one man on each arm. But she wasn't struggling, her body staggering and weak, arms limp in their grip. She was barely conscious, and I knew at once that the poor girl had been drugged, perhaps to the point of overdose.

*What do these people care?* I couldn't help ask myself. *Her health can't be any concern of theirs any more than my health could be, or Jim's.* These people had devious intentions, and this languid captive was at the heart of it.

Something about her struck me as familiar, but I couldn't place it. I knew I shouldn't trust myself, that my perception was flawed, unreliable. But I had little else to go on but my own instinct and Jim's. Together, we'd have to get to the bottom of it, or we'd sink to the bottom.

Another man bent down and grasped her ankles, holding them together with his big, gloved hands as the three men lifted her and set her on the stone slab. She groaned from under her mask, head lolling, too tired to fight, perhaps for her very life.

*Is that ... is it Kendall,* I asked myself, *Mandy's friend?*

*It's possible, they're not far off. And she's from right here in New Orleans, where at least one of the founding chapters of the cabal was located. Does she have something to do with all this? Is this second property her parents' property? Could they be living a secret life I'd never imagined, drawing us all into their web of lust and depravity?*

But something about it didn't feel right. There was a curve to the young body I recognized without realizing it and without realizing why. She rose her hips a bit, knees lifting as she tried with dwindling energy to free her ankle from the man's grip.

The pendant on the chain around her neck fell from her robe to hang over the side of her shoulder, a red ruby heart mounted in white gold. It was instantly familiar as the same pendant I was wearing, that I'd been wearing all along, the pendant we shared.

*That's why she's so familiar,* I realized in a shocked thrush of terror. My arm stretched out, my other hand clenching Jim's, almost crushing it. "Amanda … no!"

I led Jim straight into the crowd, shoving the big, robed thugs aside. Some backed away, but others converged on us. Lacking any clear leadership, they responded with defensive intent, unwilling to fall short of their duty to protect the cabal, with their lives if necessary but with Jim's and my life more realistically.

Jim was quick to pull off his mask just as I did my own, and I used mine as a weapon to smash it into the face of the man nearest me who wasn't already backing off. He shook it off, but protected by his own hard mask, the man merely fell back without losing his footing.

Jim pulled one guy's mask off as he reached out and grabbed Jim's arms. Once his face was revealed, Jim head-butted the man, snapping back with a single strike. Jim grabbed my hand again and we both pushed through the crowd toward the altar. It only seemed to get farther away as we inched our way to it, hands reaching out to grab my robe, pulling at my hair, fingers craning to grab my arms, my face, my throat.

Somebody managed to grab hold of my arm, pulling me away from Jim's side. I screamed out in a panic and leaned back. But I was no shrinking violet. I felt the power of Lizzie inside me, lashing out with an animal hiss. I pulled her leg back and, with an impassioned war cry, threw the flat sole of my foot into the man's gut. He bent forward and let go, stumbling away as Jim led me up to the altar.

We arrived at the altar and I threw myself over Amanda's body, tearing the mask away from her face. She was groggy, eyes barely opening, a groan leaking up out of her throat. I slapped her on the cheek to bring her around, rasping her name despite the din of confusion and anger and upset around us.

The crowd closed in. But Jim was a flurry of defensive moves, grabbing one of the masked goons and throwing him into the throngs, several of them tumbling back. It was good, but it wouldn't be good enough. It held them off for a moment, but it wouldn't last long.

If that was the best we could do, the three of us were as good as dead.

But Jim pulled a handgun from behind his robe, big and black and shiny. He pointed it at a nearby patch of grass and shot once into the ground, harmless but shocking, the crowd gasping and stumbling back.

*Jim must have suspected something*, I realized, *or had some reason to carry his gun with him, something he almost never does*. I was just as shocked to hear the gun shot as everyone else at that point, but grateful nonetheless.

*Thank God,* I had to think, *thank God he's here, prepared, that he's even one step ahead of me! I should have known. Jim, my James Dean, magnificent man.*

Jim turned the gun on them, jutting from one quadrant of the crowd to another, ready to take the head off the next person who flinched.

Nobody did.

Ted and Sam approached slowly, taking off their masks, calm expressions on their friendly faces.

Ted said to Jim, "Take it easy, Jim. Nobody needs to get hurt here."

"Ted? What are you doing with our daughter?"

"She wanted to know about it," Sam answered for her husband. "She was interested. You both were curious too at first, after all. You can hardly blame her."

"I don't blame her," I said, "I blame you! You were … you've been coming after her for weeks…." Visions returned to my scattered memory, a narrative I could finally follow. "They were after her too, back in California! That's … that's where I was going that day I passed out behind the wheel, to tell them to back off, leave my daughter alone. That's … what are you all thinking, coming after our little girl?"

"She's a grown woman," Sam said. "We brought you in and you loved it. There wasn't any reason not to invite Amanda as well."

"Not against her will," Jim said. "That's kidnapping, that's rape!"

"Nobody has touched your daughter," Ted said, his voice a ringing baritone of instant offense and authority. "And she's here of her own volition."

"How?" I shouted. "You got to her through her friend, is that it?"

"No," Sam said with sadly sympathetic brows. "Through

you! Don't you remember?"

All faces turned to me, those bare and those still masked. I could feel the shroud of doubt cloaked over me, the better to smother me and the truth I was revealing. It was true that I couldn't remember exactly what my early days with the cabal had been like, but I didn't need to know. That was me. That was a choice I'd made for myself, whatever Jim had to say about it, whatever part he may have played. I was ready to take responsibility for my own mistakes, even if I had to pay for them with my life.

But not Amanda.

I knew at once that I'd made some reckless decisions with my life. Whether it was symptomatic of my disease, I couldn't tell. But I knew how Jim was trying to help me enjoy my life while I still could. I knew that he would have allowed me this indulgence.

But this wasn't the life I wanted for Amanda, I knew at once. *For me, it doesn't matter, but Amanda ... she's what matters now, now and forever!*

"We know about your condition," Sam said to me. "This is just part of your sad decline, my friend."

I looked at Amanda in my arms, barely conscious. "Does this look like a figment of my imagination? Don't try to trick me! You know I'm not sure of things right now, not on my feet. You people have used that to take advantage of me, to come after my daughter without me realizing it; to manipulate me, twist me around your little fingers if you ever got caught."

"And that time has come," Jim said, turning his gun on Ted. "My daughter's friend, is she here?"

Sam shook her head. "She didn't want any part of it, your daughter said. Amanda came alone. She arrived a few hours ago, took the drink —"

I repeated, "Took the drink?"

"You've had it too," Sam said with an innocent shrug. "It's just a … a relaxant."

Jim glanced around. "I've heard enough! You're going to tell your little army here to back off and let us walk peacefully out of here."

Ted and Sam glanced at one another, the others glued to their reactions. The entire yard was focused on them. Even the women in the cages were looking on, hands clutching the bars in front of them like sad monkeys.

Ted said, "Just take it easy, Jim, reconsider from our point of view —"

"We don't care about your point of view!" I shouted.

"It's not what you think," Ted said to us both. "We mean none of you any harm. Jim, we're your friends, your *best* friends!"

Sam added, "You're here as our guests, after all!"

"So we could stand here and watch you defile our daughter?" I spat out, "Big shock you made no mention of it!"

"My wife's right," Jim said. "What you've done here is … it's unforgivable. Neither my wife nor my daughter nor I want anything to do with any of you. Never contact us again … not for any reason."

Ted held out his hands, palms flat to appease us. "Now Jim, Beth Ann, just give us a minute to explain —"

"We don't need any explanation from you," Jim said, pointing the gun out over the crowd. "Just tell these bastards to make a pathway, before I have to do it for them."

Sam said, "You can leave anytime you want, Jim, of course. We're not keeping you here! But we'd hate for you to leave with the wrong impression."

"Too late for that," I said. "We know just who you are and

precisely what you want!"

Sam said, "Do you?" I waited, a bit confused, before she went on, "Don't you remember why you wanted to come here tonight?"

"Yes, to …" But I couldn't remember, and Sam could tell that, everybody could. "What matters is that I'm here now, and I'm not letting you touch my daughter!"

"But you wanted it," Sam said. "You were so excited when you arrived."

"I changed my mind!"

But Sam looked at me with sympathy, even empathy. "Poor, deluded Beth Ann. There's nothing we want from you … other than, perhaps, your continued confidence."

Jim and I shared a woeful glance, our frowns telling the other what each one knew was coming.

Ted picked up where Sam left off. "There are a lot of good people here tonight, and we've never hurt anyone, never done anything illegal. You yourself have been a willing participant for a long time now, Beth Ann. We're both so sorry you don't remember it, or so many other things —"

"Stop bringing that up," I yelled. "Stop trying to use that against me! I know who I am and I know who you are! Nothing's going to change that."

But an even darker pallor fell over the crowd.

"Still," Ted said, "you're welcome to leave here and never return, if that's what you want. We only hope you'll pay us the same consideration, the same respect —"

I couldn't help but repeat, "The same respect? You were going to gang rape our daughter —"

"She's here voluntarily —"

"Drugged up like a zombie! And you dare to talk to us about respect? Are you insane? You think *I'm* out of *my* mind!"

I helped Amanda off the slab, her exhausted head falling onto my shoulder, her arm wrapped over me, her feet sliding from under her. Jim led us away from the altar and toward the doorway that would lead us back into that isolated corridor. Freedom waited for us, but only on the other side.

And it was by no means certain. Even if we made it out of there alive, I knew we'd be marked for death. Our enemies had power beyond imagining. No place would truly be safe from their reach. But if we could get out of New Orleans, we could fall back, make a new plan, maybe go somewhere new, someplace the Velvet Elite wouldn't care to follow. But that was still far in our uncertain futures, and we didn't even know for sure that we'd have one to share. If so, the only way to it was through that corridor. We had no choice but to fight our way back to the lives we knew if we were ever going to be able to return to them.

# CHAPTER 18
## Resolutions

Jim pointed the gun at Ted and gestured it toward himself. "You're coming with us."

Sam cried out, "Jim, no!"

Ted asked us, "Are you … are you kidnapping me?"

Jim walked to Ted and grabbed his collar, pulling him along while I was supporting Mandy's nearly dead weight. Jim said, "Just bringing you along until we get safely out of here."

Jim and I led Ted and Mandy into the stone tomb. I went in first and Jim covered us from the rear.

Once in that hole, musty and dark, Jim said, "Light the torch." Ted scrambled to do as he was told, finally flicking a lighter to the torch to illuminate the darkness. In that flickering loom, we pushed down the hallway under the boundaries between the two houses.

Ted said, "You don't have to do all this. We're just … we're just enthusiasts, that's all."

"Enthusiasts," I sneered at him as we approached the end of the corridor, our voices echoing. "I warned you against involving my daughter, I know I did."

"We never heard anything about that, Beth Ann, I swear it. Last time we talked about it, you thought it was a good idea. Don't you remember? You wanted me to call you Lizzie?" That had the ring of truth, which echoed with doubt in my heart and soul. *No,* I told myself, *that's just what this sick bastard wants!* He went on, "I never would have contacted her if I'd known you felt that way." I had to think back to the day I'd wound up on the side of the road. *I'd been on my way*

*to the local chapter to warn them away from Amanda, I know
I was. But ... I never made it. Maybe I never did tell them to
stay away from her?*

We stepped out of the corridor on the other side, Ted
saying, "Hold on a minute," so he could douse the torch, head
down in a metal cone for later use. "All right then," Ted went
on in an impatient tone. "Give a guy a gun, he's Dirty Harry
all the sudden."

We pushed through the crowd, the shocked guests backing
up, hands raising as they shared frightened glances. Jim
cleared a path, dragging Ted while I dragged Mandy, her arm
wrapped over my shoulder.

We made it into the house, the string players seeing us and
scraping to a discordant stop. People gasped to see that lethal
weapon, poised and ready to explode in a red burst of death
for one or more of any of them.

My heart was pounding, my mouth was dry. But my mind
was clear, my focus was sharp, my body was strong as I
supported my poor, drugged daughter through that house and
out the front door. There were guards, but they stepped back
to see the gun, and Ted in Jim's grip.

Jim said, "Just take it easy," as he led us down the
driveway. "It's the black Tesla," he said, one of the guards
nodding to the red-jacketed valet, who scurried off. Jim
pulled Ted close as Sam came out the front door. "Thanks for
a swell evening, Ted. I hope you and Sam are very happy
here, for years to come. But we'll never be seeing each other
again, is that clear?"

"Crystal clear, Jim." Ted swallowed hard as the valet
delivered our car. "We wish you three nothing but the best,
Jim. No, um, no hard feelings, eh?"

I helped Amanda into the car and glared at Ted and Sam as
Jim shoved Ted into Sam's arms and climbed into the driver's

side and slammed the door. The motor still running, Jim slammed the transmission into reverse. He stepped on the gas and the car jutted backward. With a hard crank of the wheel, the car spun, and a hard hit on the brakes brought it to a skidding halt, now facing forward. Another stomp on the accelerator made the sedan jump forward, tires screaming as they leapt into their escape, tearing down the long driveway and pouring recklessly onto the street, a car swerving and screeching to a stop to avoid a collision as we disappeared into the Garden district.

# CHAPTER 19
## Escape

Amanda came to her senses without any ramifications. Once we were in our Tuscan villa, four months later, a calmness returned to the family. Mandy was humble as she shuffled around the rooms and the yard, Layla by her side, licking her hand and seeking the petting and scratches they both enjoyed so much.

We spent a few uneasy days watching her regain her strength. Her usually buoyant manner was replaced, humility giving her the aura of new maturity and perspective.

"It was just … it was so strange," Amanda said over a lovely and quiet dinner, while Jim and I listened. White wine was served by candlelight, an antique lace tablecloth lending an elegance to the table, the chicken Marsala sweet and delicious. "They invited me to the party, said you'd be glad to see me. We were having a drink and things got all weird … I was so disoriented…."

I wrapped my arms around her shoulders and pulled her close. "I know, honey, believe me, I know. You don't have to be afraid anymore, honey. You're home now."

Amanda looked at me, her eyes watering, her lower lip quivering before she threw herself into my arms, tears and sobs pouring out of her and onto my shoulder. Jim and I glanced at one another, but my attention was drawn to my daughter, sobbing in my arms, more a clinging little girl than a burgeoning young woman.

"I'm so sorry, Mommy," she said, at once pushing out the words and unable to hold them back. "I … I … I'm *sssssssooooo ssssoorrrryyyyy* …"

I stroked the back of her head and pulled her close, my voice low and soothing. "*Shshshshsh*, baby, it's okay, you don't have to be sorry."

"Yyyyes, I … I do, Mommy, I do!"

"It wasn't your fault," Jim said. "They tricked you, Ted and Sam."

"But I wanted to do it, I went along with what they said they wanted to do. I drank their stupid drug wine."

"That's how they get you," Jim said. "They did the same thing to us. They trick you into wanting it, into thinking it's your idea."

Jim said, "We should have set a better example and stayed away from all that mess ourselves."

"No, honey," I felt I had to say. "It was my fault. I … I don't know why I was so drawn to it, but … but I know you were only indulging me. But I'm done with it now, we all are!"

"Thank heavens."

"No, it's … it's not that, Daddy." Amanda turned back to me, her eyes watery and round, brows arching. "I … I ran away, I ran away from you because you were sick! But I should have stayed, I never should have run off like that!"

"No, it's okay," I said. "I understand —"

"It's not okay," Amanda shouted, her voice cracking, scolding herself and not us, her recrimination directed mercilessly inward. "It'll never be okay!"

Jim said, "Baby, we … we agreed that it was a reasonable thing that you should enjoy your college years, that this wasn't a good environment for you."

"And we were right," I had to say, "with the cabal and everything. Sounds strange to say, but considering how things went, I almost wish you'd stayed away. You'd have been a lot safer."

"No, Mom, no, we were wrong! We should never be separated, and I should never have been so selfish and stupid and shortsighted ... God, I hate myself!"

"Mandy, honey —"

"But I'll never do it again," Amanda said, burying her face in my chest. "Never again." I held her tight, rocking her gently. She stared out into her memory, sniffling, pressing her face against me. "I was so ... so confused, so lost, I ... I felt something like the way you must feel ... and I was afraid, Mommy, I was so afraid."

"*Shshshshsh*, I know, honey, I know."

"But ... but it's more than that, Mom. I ... I was afraid before, I was afraid when I left in the first place."

Jim repeated, "Afraid? Of the cabal?"

Amanda shook her head, wiping a tear on my collar. "No, I was afraid of getting sick, like you are, of what was going to happen to me. I read up, I know it's ... it's hereditary. And I was afraid of what I was seeing, what was waiting for me. So I just wanted to run away from it, hoping if I didn't see it, it wouldn't be true, it wouldn't happen, like I could run away from it. But I can't, Mommy, just like you can't. It's inside us, isn't it?"

"Not necessarily, Amanda, no. Sometimes that happens, but it's not a certainty, not at all."

"Of course not," Jim said with a reassuring smile.

"It doesn't matter," Amanda said. "I still ran away, I still abandoned you. But I'll never do that again, Mommy, I promise. I'll never abandon either one of you again!" Jim reached out and stroked the back of her head. She panted, breath shallow, sniffling through her tears.

My heart nearly burst with joy as I pulled my daughter close. I wanted to speak but couldn't, my tears answering for me.

\*

March had just begun and spring was bursting out all over those gorgeous rolling foothills.

The villa was two floors of gorgeous red tile, arches, balconies that overlooked the peninsula, the glistening Mediterranean Sea meeting the royal blue sky at that distant point on the horizon. The foothills between were caked with cypress trees, tall and strong, olive and fig trees stretching their branches out into the open air, clean and fresh and untouched by mankind's industrial nightmare.

A winding road led us to the little village nearby, where lazy afternoons were spent drifting from shop to cafe, lingering over handmade end tables and lamps, the work of local masters, drinking wines that could hardly be found in the United States.

*How different life is here*, I'd thought on those long, languid excursions. Gone was the leering indignity of the Velvet Elite, but also the crass commercialization of having a strip mall on every corner, scrolling neon headlines in every downtown of every city, each a miniature Times Square.

*Life is different in Tuscany, everything is different.*

Yet there was a similarity to Northern California, the two regions sharing even a lateral orientation on the Earth itself; similar climate, similar topography, both gorgeous, breathtaking. There was also a lingering sense of purity, organic flavors and colors to the fresh fruits and vegetables. We were living as a family, enjoying the best of life, the finest foods. Yet our life felt humble, the extravagances of our events with the Velvet Elite behind us, the dark complexities having no place in our more humble, simplistic life.

It was refreshing and nostalgic, bringing back memories and warmer feelings of glad times, youth, prospects rich and full and spreading out in front of us.

*If only* ... I heard myself say in the back of my brain.

I turned to see Amanda standing with Layla at her side, gazing out over the valley while the dog barked happily at her side.

There were other things that remained the same in Tuscany, and one of them was Amanda. She was returning to her old self, healing from the fright and scars of her experiences with the VE, though she still didn't want to talk about it. But the sunniness of her disposition returned, the vivaciousness of a pretty young woman, about to be embraced by the world, desired by most and targeted by some.

But she had matured, blossomed, and when I looked at her frolicking in our Italian garden with Layla, I was struck by how much she seemed like some wild nymph, less a human than some fabled creature, at one with nature, too good for any mere mortal, fit only for a demigod.

Or better.

But even in Tuscany there were no ancient gods to come down from Olympus and take a human bride. But there were plenty of swarthy Mediterranean young men whose attentions were instantly and inextricably drawn to her flashing eyes, bright smile, a body that was young womanhood made manifest. They smiled and flirted, using their best lines on her and their worst, buying her drinks and thinking they had something a girl like her had never seen before.

But Amanda had faced down sexual depravities the like of which none of those boys could even imagine, much less match, and I was glad of it. I wanted normalcy for her, clumsy boys who only encouraged greater searching, a richer life. Amanda had a long way to go, and I wanted her to enjoy every step of the journey.

I closed my eyes and tried to remember, to savor every

recollection, every moment we spent together. Opening my eyes, I took in the blue sky, the fluffy white clouds, a perfect painting of God's creation. It was a place of magic and memory, a place I knew I'd come back to again and again throughout my life, whatever that life was to hold or for however long … or brief.

I said, "It's gorgeous, really, just beautiful."

Jim wrapped his arm tighter around my shoulder, looking at me with warm, loving eyes. "It is when you're here."

He kissed me, long and loving, an endless commitment.

Amanda cleared her throat. "Okay, well, kissing is fine, but after twenty seconds, it's just gross." Jim and I shared a chuckle, Layla barking playfully.

But the hairs stood up on the back of my neck and I glanced around, back at the hills behind and around us.

Jim asked, "What is it, hon?"

But I knew I couldn't trust my own perception, even then. I still had my disease to work through, and I knew it would be creeping up on me in unexpected ways. Even with all I knew, I was certain of all that I didn't know, and all that I might soon forget.

But there were some things I *did* know for sure. The Velvet Elite lingered, many of them remaining out there in the world. They remained, free and in power, despite our best efforts. We'd always known we couldn't destroy the entire secret society, I'd never intended to do that. But I had wanted to protect my daughter from them, from their plan to sacrifice her. I could never have known of such a plan without objecting, I knew then, without making a move against them. Those liars had been manipulating me to get to my daughter, confusing me, turning me against myself. I began to wonder if my mental dysfunction didn't have something to do with the society itself. *Could something in the drugs have affected me somehow,* I began theorizing, *caused my dementia? Is that why I was so dead set against Mandy taking part? Does that mean there could still be a cure?*

Jim glanced around, giving it some thought, then shrugging. "*Bella Italia!*"

Then something struck me, Layla's barking a vague reminder. "Oh, we have to get some of those lovely olives for dinner."

Jim snapped his fingers. "That's right! No problem, I'll take a quick drive to the village. Anything else we need?"

I didn't have to think about it for too long. Really, we had everything we needed. But there were other things we needed, I needed, things that couldn't be bought in any store. I'd narrowly escaped New Orleans with my daughter. That meant I was still capable, still able. And I wanted to stretch that capability, to make the most of it while I could.

Maybe even make more of it.

"Y'know what? Give me the keys, I'll go." Both Jim and Mandy looked at me, quietly worried, heads turning, brows crimping. "C'mon, I'm not a little kid!"

"We know that, Mom … obviously! I mean, I'm not even a little kid!"

We shared a loving chuckle. "Really, I … it's the middle of the day, the place is just a few miles down the road…."

"A very winding road," Jim said.

I tilted my head, face down, looking up at him from under my brows. "I'll bring my phone. You don't hear from me, you can call."

Without waiting for an answer, I turned and scooped up the keys. Jim called out, "Green, not black!"

I said, "I'll get both!" before pulling the front door open and letting it close behind me.

I climbed behind the wheel of the Fiat feeling

comfortable, able, strong. I'm Beth Ann Dean, damn it, nobody messes with me! I turned the engine over and hit the road leading down to the village.

As I drove, I couldn't help but think about the event which had led me to that spot; the narrow escape from New Orleans, the reunion with Amanda, my rediscovery of myself after a tussle with Lizzie, my initial impulse to drive out to keep the VE away from Amanda. It all made sense, tying together in a neat little knot, tied nice and tight.

The only problem was, that knot seemed to be tightening around my throat. I suddenly felt that I couldn't breathe, my heart pounding in my chest. My ears became a dull hum, my eyesight going in and out.

I knew the feeling instantly as the same one which had overcome me when I drove away from our house back in California, a sudden and disorienting confusion that pulsed into my brain, blotting out all instinct and reason, fear and confusion and worry and wonder, all things and everything until there was nothing at all, just a quick thrush of blackness to wash over me like a terrible tide, like the cloak of death, the endless embrace of the cold, cold ground.

*

My fingers gripped the leather steering wheel, my wrists resting on the cool steel spokes. It pushed against my forehead, cool breeze whipping through my hair. The window was open slightly or possibly broken. I woke up slowly, forcing my eyes open and focusing on the mountain terrain upended in front of me. Pushing myself away from the steering wheel and looking around, I strained to grasp what must have happened. *Did I pull over? Did I fall asleep at the wheel?*

Regaining my senses, I rolled down my squeaky and dusty window. I needed fresh air. The breeze blew through the window, sucking the air out of my lungs. I could smell the salt of the nearby ocean breeze, so I knew I couldn't be far from the water. I closed my eyes as I inhaled deeply. I looked into my rearview mirror to see the funnel of brown dust bellowing behind an approaching truck. The truck pulled up beside me and the driver leaned over to roll down the passenger side window.

"Are you okay, miss?" Still confused and a little embarrassed, I nodded. He held up his hand, "Stay right there, I'm coming around." I bobbed my head in agreement, looking around for clues as to what had happened.

Everything was intact, there was no blood anywhere, and I didn't feel any broken bones. I hadn't crashed into anything, at least I knew that. The Good Samaritan walked to my window. "Can I help you?" He repeated his question and I tried to answer him. He seemed worried, and that began to worry me, too.

A wave of heat swept through me. My heart was racing. My limbs felt foreign and uncontrolled. I raised my hands to my face. They were cold and clammy.

"Well," he said, "you seem okay. I'm glad of that." While I was enjoying his reassuring presence, I noticed he seemed every bit as shaken by the whole situation as I was. It couldn't have been every day he found a confused passed-out woman in a car on the side of the road.

He wiped his hand on his jeans and pushed his baseball cap up slightly. He was a ruggedly handsome man, tall, built, dark hair, dark eyes, and an olive complexion. He held out his hand to shake mine. "Ted."

## THE END

EXCERPT from CLAN OF THE SHE BEAR:
Diamonds in the Rough

PART 1: Hannah Alexander
CHAPTER ONE
Marion County, Indiana 1840

The mountain seemed quiet. Hannah felt as if she were right there with them, transported fifty years back in time, but only a few precious miles away, her old friend's words echoing in her imagination.

"They worked from before dawn," old man Roth said, his voice grainy, "that day like every day. Their cruel master would have nothing less, and his pitiful slaves could offer up no more. They all knew a day would come when things would have to change. And though the mountain seemed quiet that morning … " His words trailed off and a chill ran through Hannah's body. She was safe in her neighbor's house, standing by his bed, her loving family in the house next door. But Hannah felt as if she were a slave, shuffling through that freezing mud and into that endless hole, deeper and deeper into the ground.

Whale oil lamps flickered against the round, jagged walls and ceilings of the mine, the shovels digging into the hard rock in a continuous rattle, underscored by the slaves' grunts and panting, air becoming thin.

"But the foreman had gotten word from the master himself. They were to drive deeper into the mountain, further down, the angle too sharp for a cart and rail, a canal that would suck men down to their deaths for certain."

Hannah's eyes widened, mouth dipping in horrified suspense, the light of Roth's own lamp flickering against his papered walls.

"But the master, his name was Chisholm, Cyrus Chisholm as I recall, told the foreman, 'To the devil with them'!

"The foreman tried to explain the expense of losing so many slaves," Roth told Hannah. "How much time they'd lose having to get to the slave market, but Chisholm wouldn't hear it." In another voice, more stern and parental, angry and blustery, Roth enacted the part of Cyrus Chisholm, the slave master and the property owner, the man behind the massive mining project.

"'What good are they to me if their labor fails to bring me the results I'm looking for? If there's a shortage of labor, get more! Send some of your men out to collect more numbers, if that's what you need — '

"'But master,' the foreman said,'" Roth went on in the more careful voice of the foreman, "'the roads are dangerous. And without enough guards on our force here, they could rebel — '"

"'Then I'll kill them all myself,' Chisholm shouted back. 'I want those diamonds, and I'll drag every one of those coal-skinned bastards to the gates of hell by the very scruff of the neck to get them!'"

Hannah stood by Roth's bed, almost afraid of the old man who'd become her friend and confidant. No longer the harmless, hairless old man down the road, he'd embodied the fearful fiend of his tale. His story, and his performance, had that strong a grip on her imagination.

And it was only beginning.

Roth went on. "So the foreman drove the slaves deeper into the mountain, digging farther into the darkness, carrying dirt and rock up in buckets. The tunnels became so sharp and so narrow that men were cutting into their own bare feet with their rusty spades as they dug, stifling their own screams to avoid being cut down by the other slaves just to keep the foreman from coming down on them all. There was no air, no light, men pressed against each other, no room to dig or to move."

"'Get on with it,' the foreman shouted, 'dig, you Godless savages!'"

In Hannah's imagination, the mountain no longer seemed so quiet.

The rumbling came in long and slow, creeping in under the growling and straining breathing, shovels clanking against the hard rock. But once that distant rumble got louder, leaking into the first ear and then the other, all other sounds came to a stuttering stop. Shovels ceased, those who could still breathe held that breath, knowing it could be their last.

The rumbling brought the shaking, clumps of dirt and rock falling from the ceilings and walls. Then the screaming began. The foreman said nothing, already on his way to a cowardly escape, leaving his workers to die. And their terror clamored against the walls of the trembling mine, wooden beams cracking in the upper tunnels as the slaves trampled over each other toward the exit.

They clawed at each other in deathly panic, shoving their brethren aside, vicious and desperate in a drive to escape, to survive.

But the lower tunnels, so fresh and so raw, unsupported and slick, were filled with men scrambling from the water as it rose up from the sopping base. They climbed on top of one another, hands reaching up in clawed finality as their heads were shoved into the muddy water, last air bubbles rising up and bursting.

Dead.

Several managed to pull themselves up to one of the main tunnels, and those poor souls were trampled by others racing to safety, some of them falling with shattered ankles or knees to writhe in the mud, destined to die along with the others.

"The rumbling and the shaking only got worse," Roth told Hannah, his old, yellowed eyes wide, bony fingers craned in front of him to bring his tale to life. "One of the lower tunnels broke from the bottom out, water pouring in from an underground spring. And it flooded the chambers quickly, roaring like a freight train down those main tunnels, drowning every poor living soul still in a lower chamber. Those still running in the upper tunnels, feet slipping in the mud, some of them fool enough to turn and see the face of the charging death that came up behind them, frozen in fear, finally accepting what they knew they couldn't ever have denied … their fate."

Hannah stood by that bed, unable to move. "W-w-w-w-what happened?"

Old man Roth went on. "They say the foreman made it out … some say anyway."

"But … the slaves?"

"All dead, s'what the townsfolk said, all drowned. Some people even started saying the mine was haunted."

"Haunted?"

"Well sure, Hannah, sure! There are spirits, some say, a lot of people. You believe in God, don't cha?"

"Of course I do!"

"Of course you do," Roth repeated with a tender smile on his cracking face, his old, chilly hands finding Hannah's, young and supple. "So you believe in a soul, right?" Hannah only had to nod, and Roth went on, "And you know that black folks, they got souls too, just like white folks, right? Yer not one of those people think that ain't so, not you."

Hannah shook her head. "If God made them, and they're people, they must have souls."

160

"That's right, Hannah," Roth said, a little tear rolling down his cheek, "that's very, very right. And what do you think happens when a soul can't find a way to heaven somehow, because they're trapped somewhere, or are sad or confused and can't find God's light, or ... or they just can't rest in peace, maybe because they were so wronged in their lives, Hannah, so much pain that they just can't let go of."

Hannah had never known such pain, and Roth could see it in her eyes. She knew his little smile was a grateful smile, that he was glad she could hardly guess what horrors those poor souls must have endured. He hoped she never would, and even at ten years old, Hannah hoped so, too.

"Anyways," Roth said, "the waters went down, back into the mountain, and the townsfolk finally made old man Chisholm dynamite the mountain, close up the mine."

"Because of the ghosts?"

Roth nodded. "Some say, others 'cause there weren't no diamonds anyway."

"Were there? Diamonds, I mean."

Roth looked at her, long and slow, leaning forward a little bit, a glint in his eye. "Not that they ever found. 'Course the legend is that the spirits, they're still workin' the mine, been workin' it all this time. Sometimes the mountains shake a bit, some folks think thats thems hittin' a vein, openin' up a new tunnel, goin' even deeper. Deeper and deeper and deeper ... deep into the ground ... "

Old man Roth lay back into his pillow, his fragile, knobby hands slipping out of Hannah's, falling to his sides and then slowly rising up to fold over his chest, rising slowly with his wheezing breath.

"Always wanted to find that mine myself," Roth said, "always wanted to believe it was true. But it wasn't ... " His words trailed off with a few sputtering coughs.

"It wasn't … it wasn't real?"

He looked at her with a gentle smile and a last flicker of light in his eyes. "It wasn't … my fate."

Hannah stood by the bed as old man Roth closed his eyes and leaned further back into his pillow. "Go on back home now, Hannah, it's time for your supper." Hannah nodded and stepped away from the bed. "You'll come back, visit me again tomorrow."

"My mom's made some prickle berry jam."

"You'll bring me some?"

"A whole big jar," Hannah said, "just for you."

Roth smiled. "For us, Hannah. We'll share it … we'll share it all."

# EXCERPT from FRUITS OF THE VINE

## CHAPTER ONE
### *Lamezia Terme, Italy 1934*

Pia Stracci peeked up from behind the bar as the soldier's voice grew louder in the café's main room. His rising, drunken anger cut through the steam, and smells of olive oil, clams and lemon, hot and thick around her.

"Stracci, you bandit," one of them shouted, nearly knocking the table over as he stood, chest out and shoulders back. "We'll not pay a lira!"

Pia's mother, Constanza, ran out from the kitchen, unable to stay behind or remain silent any longer. The few customers who remained sat frightened, contemplating their hasty retreats as soon as could be managed.

But for Miguel Stracci, there was no running away and no more backing down. Pia knew that, and she knew in her little eight-year-old heart what it would bring. Constanza had warned him about it countless times in an urgent rasp, their native Italian peeling off her terrified tongue.

And as Miguel and the officers of the *Opera Vigilanza Repressione Antifascism* quickly passed the lines of civility and sobriety, Pia knew that her mother had been right.

"IIow can you refuse to pay?" Miguel asked, holding the bill in his hand, pointing to it and then to the café around him, "and then take arms against the so-called socialists? You're as good ... or as bad ... as they are!"

The bigger soldier drew up his rifle, stock ready to smash into Miguel's face. But Pia's father stood there, unafraid, unwilling to be pressured by the black-shirted men of Mussolini's Organization for Vigilance against Anti-Fascist Activities.

"Please, just go," Constanza pleaded with the soldiers.

"We don't lay down," Miguel said, his eyes fixed on them. "Not anymore!"

"Miguel!"

But Miguel ignored her, staring down the soldiers. "I have a family of my own to feed! I can't support the whole of Lamezia Terme."

One of the soldiers, who Pia had heard her father refer to as Valletti, shook an angry finger in Miguel's face. "You ungrateful swine! *Il Duce* has brought you roads and churches and hospitals! He and he alone can bring Italy back to its former greatness."

"Italy will always be great," Miguel said. "She was before *Il Duce* and will be long afterward, after us all!"

The two soldiers glanced at each other, then at the cowering customers around them. Miguel Stracci's patriotism had never been in question, and for him to say such a thing not only impressed the soldiers, but it seemed to humble them because silence replaced their clapping voices.

"You dare to speak that way of *Il Duce*?" Salvatore said, his body beyond his own ability to control, pulling toward Miguel and ready to strike. "I'll make an example of you and this entire place!"

The crowd gasped, their fear notable and only curling in Pia's own stomach. However afraid they were, they were many times her age, height and weight. Her fear was the only thing greater than theirs.

But it was Valletti's staying hand that kept Pia's fear from erupting out of her mouth in a terrified scream. "Salvatore, you're too quick to anger—"

"And you're too slow to correct! These swine have got to learn!"

THE VELVET ELITE: Unforgettable Love / Waterford

"And learn they will, Salvatore." Valletti turned to Miguel and Constanza, addressing everyone in the room, even Pia, who had quietly crawled from the bar to hide in the kitchen. "They will learn that Benito Mussolini is a man of the people, a man of the land!" After a dramatic pause, he added, "He is a man of this people, a man of this land … Italy, beautiful Italy. *bella Italia*!"

Tension filled the room, only getting thicker, even as the soldier's words and tone took a friendlier course.

"*Il Duce* would never seek to harm one of his own, not ever; of that, you can all be certain. He loves you …" Valletti turned back to Miguel, looking him up and down with a disgusted sneer. "Even the foolish among you, even the willful. If you can turn that will to the causes of his favor, having more children and lending your back and your brain to the betterment of our society, what reason would *Il Duce* have to punish you? And what reason would you—would any of you—have to defy him?"

No answer came back, only frightened silence and beguiled loyalty. Valletti said to his partner, "Salvatore, perhaps we should pay this fine Italian merchant what he deserves, eh?"

Salvatore looked at Miguel with a knowing grin and a slow nod. "Perhaps we should, indeed."

Constanza clung to Miguel, standing behind his protective shoulders, his chest and chin jutted to refute their military authority with every contemptuous breath. Salvatore and Valletti took in his quiet determination, his swelling sense of pride.

Valletti cleared his throat and addressed Miguel. "Our apologies, *Signore* Stracci. But we must admit that we haven't the funds on hand. We shall return tomorrow and deliver the total to you in full … with my assurances that such a thing will never … ever … happen again."

The men stared each other down, the soldiers finally offering the Stracci's a nod and a slight smile before turning to take their leave. Pia ran and threw herself into her parents' arms, the three Straccis' clinging to each other with love, gratitude and desperate relief.

~~~

Pia couldn't get her mind off the faces of Salvatore and Valletti, their evil smirks. *Why would they be so respectful? They're so ready to discipline, why let us alone in such a public way?*

But her brain began to hurt from wondering, the rest of her body tired from the rush of fear and the subsequent tension in the café and their little rooms just above it. Pia felt as if she could hear the rats talking about the danger, scurrying to lay low and stay out of *Il Duce*'s wrath.

Pia knew she and her family didn't have that option.

The rooms were filled with the smells of the dinners and drinks they'd served, heavy red wines, garlic, hard cheeses and more pageant soft varieties. But the voices had all disappeared, both angry and frightened, and only those of Miguel and Constanza remained, trading urgent whispers.

"They'll come back tomorrow," Constanza said, "and they won't be happily paying their bill."

"Perhaps not, Connie, but what choice do we have? We'll not just abandon our home, that's just what they want! To take the café, at least for the money and liquor and food. If we didn't keep cooking and cleaning and pouring, they'd have no reason to keep us alive at all!"

"The child, Miguel!"

"Precisely so, Constanza! Should I teach her that the way of life is to cower or roll over like a dog to every thickheaded

166

man with a badge or a gun who comes along? We have a right to a better life than that, she has a right—"

"To grow up with both parents," Constanza insisted. "With you going on this way—"

"I've bent as far as I can, Connie! What's the purpose of living if not to be alive?"

"To *remain* alive!"

And so the night went until Constanza ushered Pia into bed, but not first without saying her prayers.

*Dear Lord:*

*Please keep my family and me in the safety of Your love and care. Bring my daddy peace in his mind and my mother peace in her heart, and for me, peace in our lives.*

*Pia.*

*Bam, bam, crash!* The door downstairs could only withstand three terrific blows, and the woody crunch and crack told Pia the same thing it told her parents. Cold shock shot up the child's spine as she bolted up in bed, light from the hallway leaking in through her opened door. Her father's heavier footsteps ran down the stairs as her mother scrambled frantically toward Pia's room, louder, until she burst in and fell to her daughter's bed, arms wrapped around her.

"What's the meaning of this?" Miguel hollered, but he was met with growled responses.

Pia thought she heard, "Petulant, mouthy maggot!" even as her mother held her tighter as if to blot out the horror of what she was hearing and what she surely was imagining. Indeed, Pia felt as if she was down there herself, standing with her father against the men whose voices she already recognized. She'd have known who they were even without recognizing them as Salvatore's sinister tone was emblazoned on Pia's memory. It made the stark horror of what was happening clearer in her mind's eye.

"You're under arrest," Valletti snapped at Miguel, his voice more drunken than it had been before, reason becoming a slurred snicker.

"I've done nothing other than try to make a decent living!"

"Sedition!" Salvatore shouted. Above and around her, Pia's mother jerked to get up from the bed, arms nearly letting go of Pia in a flight to join her husband. But she remained, her arms holding tight around her little daughter, body trembling and conflicting impulses that Pia knew, even at her tender age, were tearing her mother apart. Downstairs, Salvatore went on, "Dissidence, openly defying the government and its laws—"

Miguel snapped back, "Its dictator, you mean!"

"Bastard!" The wet crunch registered in Pia's gut and in Constanza's arms as she struggled again between the warring instincts to remain and protect her child or go downstairs and attempt to save her husband.

She whispered, "Stay here, child," and Pia knew she'd made her choice. Pia was struck with a sudden rush of emptiness as Constanza leapt out of the bed and seemed to fly across the room and out the door. "Miguel!"

"Get back, woman," Valletti shouted, still unseen from Pia's upstairs bedroom. "We'll take you in as well!"

"We told you we don't need your money," Constanza said, the quivering terror in her voice making Pia's stomach churn with warm nausea. "You've no need to come back here to pay —"

"The law is the law," Valletti said. "And our leader loves the law as much as he loves the people and the land. All are his, after all!" The two soldiers laughed, and from her dark enclave upstairs, Pia knew why the men had gone away and come back, to find some legal excuse, to serve both their masters' greed and their own in a way that best served them. And then, like the animals they were and not the men of authority or of law as they pretended to be, they struck in the dead of night and with lethal force.

"Don't, Constanza," Miguel said. "I'll go with these pigs … you stay and raise our child, tell her … tell her I love her."

"No, Miguel," Constanza called in horror, already sobbing through her strained throat, "you can't go with them! You'll never return—"

"I will, Connie, by the morning we'll be breaking fast together—"

"Save the storybooks for your little girl," Salvatore said. "And you, woman, you'd best gather her up and the rest of your trash and go before we return to take possession in the morning!"

Pia knew that her father had been right, that he was facing certain doom and that she and her mother would be lucky to escape with their lives if they were quick enough to do it before morning. Nobody would help them, Pia knew, none of the smiling faces of their neighbors or fellows would hide them or stand with them, not against Mussolini, not against even a single pair of his wretched Blackshirts.

But Pia also knew the men knew she was there, and there was no reason to hide. She felt the same impulse she knew Constanza had felt for Miguel, to rush to their side and stand with them, to protect if she could and die with them if not. She'd been hiding too long.

She crept out of bed, fear pulling her back even as something else inside her pushed her forward, the voices becoming louder as her tiny feet carried her into the hall.

"You can't take my husband," Constanza begged them, her figure becoming visible to Pia as she crept down the hall to the top of the stairs. In the living room beneath her,

Constanza was leaning against a table for support, her beloved Miguel already on his knees between the two soldiers, his forehead bleeding from a fresh, swelling split above the left eye. "Take the café, you'll never see any of us again, but I beg of you!"

Valletti turned to Constanza and took a few slow steps toward her. "You're a dutiful wife, a good Italian woman." He reached out, gloved fingers finding her chin. "You must have been very beautiful in your time, eh?"

Constanza cracked out a terrified gasp, withholding her whimpers as she tried to remain standing upright and proud. "Do with me whatever you wish, but spare my family—"

Valletti glanced back at Salvatore, who shared his little chuckle. Miguel was trying to push himself up from the floor, but the dizziness from his wound kept him helpless, a wounded bull ready for castration … and then slaughter.

"Very well," Valletti said with a smile. He lowered his hand from Constanza's face and took a step back, manner brisk and military as he pulled a pistol from his holster, aimed it directly at her chest, and fired once.

The blast filled the room, Constanza flying backward and out of Pia's sight even as the air was sucked from her lungs, no scream managing to escape. Her body was frozen, blood like ice, limbs able only to quiver.

Miguel reached out for her, but another hard blow to his head sent him falling straight back to the hardwood floor.

"Papa!" Pia heard her own voice cry out before she realized, her body carrying her down the stairs absent of her own will, delivering her to the hands of her family's murderers despite every reason to remain hidden, to bend, to cower.

But she just couldn't.

By the time Pia reached the bottom of the stairs, they saw her coming. Salvatore's hand cut through the air and smacked Pia hard against the right side of her head, brain rattling in her skull as her body flew halfway across the room and collapsed next to her mother's body. She reached over and clung to her mother, her hopes that she'd feel a life pulse instantly vanished upon contact with the motionless flesh. But Pia had nothing and nobody else.

"Papa!" But in turning to call to her father one last time, Pia could only focus on the blackened tip of Salvatore's pistol barrel, aimed directly at her.

But it was Valletti who shook his head and lowered the pistol in his partner's grip. "She's only a child, Salvatore."

"She'll want revenge—"

"If she were a boy, I'd agree. But …" He pointed out Pia's small frame, huddled next to her mother's corpse, already growing cold. "Let the gypsies have her." Salvatore didn't seem impressed, but his eyes shifted back to Pia and then to Valletti, and a shrug was his final answer. He holstered the pistol and stepped toward Pia, reaching instead into the vest of his pocket. He pulled out a billfold and from it, almost ten thousand lire. Dropping the bills on the floor in front of Pia, he said, "Consider this payment in full." Another few hundred lire later, he added, "And this for the funeral."

With that, Salvatore turned, and the two soldiers picked up Miguel, one taking each arm and dragging him out of the house, leaving the door open behind them.

Pia sat at her mother's side, eyes wide and staring, lips unmoving, chest still. Pia wanted to beg her mother to rise, to wake, to return to life and to her, for life to return as it was.

But she also knew it would never be. Her mother was dead. In all of Pia Stracci's eight years, this was something she'd never contemplated and simply couldn't entirely digest. Though she understood it with hideous clarity.

Her mother was dead.

But her father was alive, and the sounds of the car door closing outside proved it. He was all Pia had, and everything in her body, in her heart and in her soul, told her to go after him, not to let them take him away, not to let them kill him the way they had killed her mother.

"Papa," she said as the car engine turned over, then again called out, "Papa!" before throwing herself across the room and to the door. "Papa!"

As Pia spilled out of the front door of the café, the black sedan was pulling away, tires screeching, engine roaring. "Papa!" Pia held out her hands and ran as fast as her feet would carry her. Her bare feet slapped against the cold, hard pavement, the night air cold against her skin, nightgown and bathrobe doing little to warm her.

But inside, she was burning, on fire, almost melting as everything in her world dissolved in the same hellish way. Pia could only keep running, even as the sedan turned another winding corner, its engine became increasingly soft and distant, her father impossible to reach, to see, to save.

"Papa!" Pia kept running, the streets of Lamezia Terme quiet around her, her own voice echoing off the side of one row of buildings and then another, a pitiful cry that many could surely hear.

Nobody was answering.

But Pia was lost to them, driven forward beyond fear, beyond reason, until her body kept running only because it was all there was left to do. Though there was nowhere to run and nobody to run with, there was nothing behind her either. Her entire world shifted into a swirling vortex of doom and panic. In a few tragic hours, Pia Stracci's life had been wiped away. There was no life, there was only flight. It didn't matter where she ran to or if she ran at all. But Pia ran anyway, until her lungs couldn't find another breath, until her feet couldn't take another step.

Then she kept running.

The black of the Italian sky surrounded her, the lights of Lamezia Terme distant behind, only a lonely road to keep her company on the last few desperate miles. Her body was numb, her mind eager to dream, not even waiting for her body to rest. An owl cried somewhere above her, and Pia dreamed that she was in her bed, safe in her house, her parents smiling down on her, protective and loving, all right with the world.

Sleep now, they seemed to be saying in a soft owl's voice. *Rest with us, dear one. Lay down your flight, there's nothing to run from. You're with us now. You're home.*

Pia could almost feel the warm sheets around her, taste the happy tears of her grateful parents, sense their love as the three of them cuddled under the stars.

Resting in peace.

# ABOUT THE AUTHOR

Author Emmy Waterford is making her long-form fiction debut with *The Velvet Elite* series. Waterford creates a singularly unique romantic heroine for our time in a sexy, fast-paced romantic thriller which combines elements of the *"Fifty Shades"* series, *"Eyes Wide Shut"*, and the modern film classic, *Memento*. Her alluring writing style will leave you on the edge of your seat and begging for more.

Made in the USA
Coppell, TX
06 December 2023

25218541R00096